THE
CHRONONAUT

KYLE ALEXANDER ROMINES

The future. Millennia of scientific discovery have led to mankind's greatest feat: the invention of time travel, a technology with a potential for learning and scientific advancement rivaled only by its potential catastrophic consequences. To prevent such outcomes, the world government has carefully restricted the technology, limiting its use and study to a selected few.

Dr. Amelia Lewis is a temporal historian charged with uncovering humanity's greatest unsolved historical mysteries during her voyages into the timestream. It is on one of these missions that she witnesses something more terrifying than anything mankind has ever encountered—a monstrous entity that exists outside of time itself. Amelia's journeys into the past have drawn its gaze, and now it seeks to devour her.

As she desperately seeks a way a to save herself, Amelia discovers that everyone she cares about is being erased from existence. The fabric of her life is beginning to unravel. Soon, there may not be anything to go back to.

ALSO BY KYLE ALEXANDER ROMINES

The Keeper of the Crows (Sunbury Press)

*This novella is dedicated to anyone who has
ever wished they could go back.*

"I will dash them in pieces, I will make the memory of them to cease from among men."

—*Deuteronomy 32:26*

CHAPTER ONE

I T BEGAN WITH LIGHT. EVERYTHING faded away, and the light grew so bright she had to close her eyes. An overpowering whiteness enveloped her. The light faded as quickly as it appeared, and when Amelia opened her eyes she found herself in an infinite abyss. There was nothing around her but blackness forever, accompanied by an alien coldness that permeated the thick confines of her suit.

Her radio was dead, and there were no signs of life anywhere in sight. For a single moment in time, she was utterly alone. Her heart skipped a beat, and dread settled in the pit of her stomach. It was the same fear she felt whenever she first made the jump— the fear that something would go wrong, and she would be stuck there forever. Amelia fought back the feeling, relaxed, and waited.

She emerged from a black vortex, a hole in the fabric of space and time the scientists had designated "the gateway." She floated in front of the vortex, looking like one of the original astronauts from the 20th century. Behind her, a tether of golden light with a solid metal core was anchored to her back, disappearing into the gateway. The farther Amelia floated, the farther the tether stretched.

"Temporal flux stabilized," a voice echoed over her receiver. "Dr. Lewis, do you copy?" asked Gavin, the mission supervisor.

Amelia didn't answer. She stared across the endless expanse in front of her, seized by overwhelming awe. The walls of a circular tunnel surrounded her on all sides, stretching back to the black gateway from where she had emerged. The tunnel walls were composed of opaque, ethereal, blue light that rippled like waves crashing against a shore. The tunnel reminded Amelia of the massive subterranean aquarium her father had taken her to when she was a little girl. Smaller pockets of white light punctuated the blue expanse at random intervals, firing like neurons interspersed throughout the human brain.

She gazed across the tunnel through her helmet's visor, which also displayed a technological interface complete with readings and a communications system that allowed for the transmission of messages to and out of the timestream.

"I copy," Amelia said into her helmet's receiver. "I'm inside the timestream."

Like time itself, the tunnel stretched on, seemingly without end. The tunnel's blue walls grew darker the farther back it went. No one knew what lay at the tunnel's end. The predominant theory was it ran to the beginning of time itself, a hypothesis far too dangerous to be tested.

"Visual connection established. We're seeing what you're seeing. The mission is a go."

Amelia caught herself nodding, even though no one was around to see her. *It's time to get to work*, she thought, landing on the floor of the tunnel. The spots of blue light glowed under her feet as she walked farther along the tunnel. She punched a few buttons on the gauntlet attached to the right sleeve of her EMV, which served as a connection to her visor's interface.

"I'm moving through the timestream," she said. "I've locked onto the coordinates and am approaching the target destination."

Her EMV was form-fitted. Though padded and reinforced, it was flexible and easy to move around in, unlike the suits of her astronaut predecessors. As a student of history, Amelia felt a sense of kinship with the astronauts of old. They too had charted an unknown course into a foreign and dangerous world where few dared to tread, much like the ancient seafarers before them. Centuries had passed since the advent of interstellar flight, and mankind had long ago mastered space travel. Now there was a new frontier: time. Amelia was one of the first chrononauts, a government-sanctioned time traveler.

A sensor in Amelia's visor went off, warning her that she was fast approaching the window to her intended destination. She came to a halt and used the interface to lock onto the target. Her visor highlighted one of the countless white lights scattered across the blue waves comprising the tunnel walls. When she looked carefully, Amelia could see images through the white lights, which at close range were more similar in appearance to mirrors than lights—mirrors that served as windows into the past.

"1587 A.D.E.," Amelia said. "The Eastern Province of Continental America, formerly the state of North Carolina, formerly part of the British colony of Virginia."

"Date confirmed," said Gavin on the other end of the receiver. "Stand by while we approximate the location."

Amelia waited as the scientists studied her readings and prepared to transmit their findings back to her suit. The same routine happened every time a chrononaut traversed a portal through the timestream into the past. As she waited, her eyes drifted past the tunnel's walls to what lurked outside. Beyond the tunnel lay endless nothingness—a sea of gray and black that hung outside the timestream like a veil, existing outside of time itself. Amelia tried not to dwell on it—the idea that anything could be outside of time was hard to wrap her mind around. Then again, she was an historian, not a scientist.

The periphery of her visor lit up with yellow illumination as the scientists' data was downloaded into her suit's system.

"Dr. Lewis, you are cleared to make the jump."

"Understood," she said, returning her focus to the window. "Standby while I confirm functionality." She pressed her hand up against it, and the wall wavered against her touch. Before every jump, she always ran a final diagnostic on her suit's functionality, even though it had been thoroughly checked before she passed through the gateway into the timestream.

"My temporal stabilizers are operating at full capacity," she said, "along with the tether, valence-phaser, and communications systems."

In addition to the golden tether anchoring her to the now-distant gateway, each part of Amelia's EMV served a core function in traversing the timestream. Her temporal stabilizers kept her fixed in one place in time, allowing her to move freely through time and space. Without a stabilizer, she ran the risk of getting lost in time, which was why her suit had two—a primary stabilizer in the center of her chest and a second, smaller stabilizer on her left wrist.

"I'm disengaging the tether," she said.

Amelia put her hand on the tether where it was attached to the back of her suit and twisted it ninety degrees before pulling back on the handle. The tether slid free with a hiss.

It was the tether that allowed her to wander through the timestream while anchored to the gateway, so that she could find her way back from where she came. She couldn't take the tether with her into the past, but it was synchronized with her EMV and would rematerialize the moment she returned to the timestream.

"All right," Amelia said. "I'm making the jump."

"Good luck," Gavin replied.

Amelia pushed through the window and out of the timestream. Unlike the act of passing through the gateway, she immediately emerged on the other side, high above the earth. There were no buildings or manmade structures in sight, only forests for miles and miles. This was the planet as it had been before the Age of Industrialization, when the earth was untamed by humankind.

"Wow," she muttered into her helmet. Her suit's hovering technology held her suspended above the earth.

"What is it?" Gavin asked.

"It's nothing," she said. "I always forget how different everything looks in the past."

"I guess it's different when you're there in person," Gavin replied, and Amelia remembered he was observing on a screen everything she was seeing through her visor. "Don't forget to activate your valance-phaser before you descend," he reminded her.

Amelia twisted a dial on the back of her glove. "I'm doing it now," she said.

The device kept her out of phase with the world around her, as if she was a ghost or astral projection. She could explore the world without altering it, a core requirement for a temporal historian. It was one of the key features that distinguished her from the temporal enforcers, the chrononauts who monitored and policed the timestream. They were the only ones authorized to directly interact with the past, and only rarely at that, in order to prevent alterations to the timeline.

Time travel had been discovered years before Amelia's birth, but it had only been perfected and made safe within the last two decades. Its use was banned to the public by the world government, permitted only by the elite chrononauts selected by the agency in charge of timefaring. There were a handful of people who had attempted time travel for their own ends, using homemade technology. The temporal enforcers hunted these individuals through time and kept them from causing changes in the prime timeline.

"I'm beginning my descent," Amelia said. She looked at the reading on her display. *July 22, 1587 A.D.E.* It was the day John White and 114 English colonists reached North America, where they would eventually establish a colony at Roanoke. "I see them," she said quietly. "The colonists." Although she knew the colonists couldn't see or hear her—while out of phase she was invisible to their eyes—she found herself holding her breath anyway. "The lost colony of Roanoke," Amelia said. *This is a huge moment in historical discovery,* she thought to herself.

"We're establishing a link to the moment in time through your stabilizer," Gavin's voice echoed through her receiver. "We're also recording all the data and footage from your EMV systems."

Since the world government prevented the use of time travel to alter the past for any reason, the technology's primary purpose was in the documentation of history. By traversing the timestream, historians could now access millennia of data previously lost to the ravages of time, once thought forever forgotten.

Amelia hadn't become a temporal historian by accident; before her selection for training as a chrononaut, she was already one of the world's leading historians, despite her relatively young age. Amelia's greatest accomplishment had been observing and recording the birth, early life, and death of Alexander the Great, making her the world's foremost expert on the subject and inspiring no small amount of jealousy in her colleagues. At the moment, she was investigating the lost colony of Roanoke, another of history's unsolved mysteries.

"This is Dr. Amelia Lewis, recording the mission log for the Roanoke Project," she said, speaking into the suit's recording unit. She charted a course toward the ocean, where she knew the colonists were due to arrive. "In the year 1587 A.D.E., a group of English settlers led by John White came to the what was then considered the 'New World' to start a colony that subsequently became known as Roanoke. After conflict with the Native Americans, White returned to England to request help from the crown, leaving his family and newborn granddaughter behind. When he returned to Roanoke three years later, the settlement was abandoned. Over one hundred colonists had vanished without a trace. The only clue to their disappearance was the word *Croatoan* carved into a tree."

Standing near the forest's periphery, Amelia paused, deep in thought. Her hand hovered inches away from the bark of one of the trees, any of which could have been the tree bearing the famous message.

"Dr. Lewis?" Gavin asked over the radio, interrupting her thoughts.

Amelia resumed her mission log as she headed toward a cliff from which she could witness the settlers' arrival. "White never discovered what happened to his family. His men forced him to return to England before he had the chance to search further. The disappearance of the lost colony was a mystery that has never been solved, and over the centuries it became a hotly contested matter of debate among historians. Some believe Native Americans had wiped out the colonists. Others suspect the colonists had sought refuge with another tribe of friendlier natives." It was a debate Amelia intended to put to rest once and for all.

Gazing across the waters of the Atlantic from the rocky cliff overlooking the ocean, she watched the ship bearing the colonists approach the shore. Amelia observed their landing and followed them as they began the journey farther inland. She eagerly took note of each individual colonist, marveling in the sights and sounds of the past. When Amelia was a little girl, nothing had captivated her as much as her father's stories of the past, and her love of history only grew as she aged. To experience the past firsthand—it was beyond any historian's wildest dreams.

"We've almost synchronized our external feed with your temporal position," Gavin said, startling her. Amelia, who had been watching the settlers begin constructing new homes and shelters, was so absorbed in what she was doing she had forgotten about her monitors in the present. "Soon we'll be able to access the window remotely from the timestream."

Amelia sighed. She could spend years studying the colonists and learning their ways, but she was there on a mission. "I'm moving forward," she said, punching a series of keys on her gauntlet. Time began to flow more quickly around her, with the colonists moving faster and faster. Amelia's temporal stabilizer held her in place as the sun set and rose again in seconds, and day after day passed in the blink of an eye. Amelia stared down at the display feed on her gauntlet.

"You're approaching the date John White left for England," Gavin said.

"This is it," Amelia replied. "Everything after that is unrecorded by history." *But not for long,* she thought. She temporarily slowed the flow of time again to watch White's departure, keenly studying the look on his face as he said goodbye to his family. Amelia looked at White's infant granddaughter, the first colonist born in the New World. From White's expression, he had no idea he was seeing her for the last time. *By the time he returns, they will be long gone,* she thought, feeling a strong sense of empathy that caused her to think of her own father.

Amelia sped up time again, albeit at a slower pace. For a time, life went on as usual in the colony. "Something's going to happen soon," she said. "I can feel it."

Sure enough, she watched as a colonist hunting in the woods crossed paths with a member of a Native American tribe known as the Eno. A disagreement occurred, followed by a struggle that resulted in the native's death. When the colonist returned to Roanoke, Amelia sped up time again, but she didn't have to wait long. The Eno began launching attacks on the colonists, picking them off one by one when they strayed from the settlement and eventually growing bold enough to launch raiding parties.

Amelia followed along as the colonists sought shelter with the natives living on a nearby island known as Croatoan.

"They survived," Amelia said with a smile. She sped up time

again and watched as the settlers intermarried with the natives, and then Amelia returned to Roanoke for John White's return. She saw the pain on his face when he discovered his family missing, and she heard the emotion in his voice as he attempted to convince his men to allow him to search for them. Amelia, who knew he was destined to fail, decided she had seen enough.

"That's it," she said. "The mystery of the lost colony has finally been laid to rest."

She heard clapping in the background over the receiver. "Congratulations, Dr. Lewis. I look forward to reading about your findings in more detail."

Amelia typed in a series of keys into her gauntlet. "I'm reentering the timestream," she said.

Tether engaged, flashed a message from her suit's A.I. across her visor, and Amelia felt herself again pulled through space and time.

She emerged through the window as if passing through a cloud. Amelia stood once more inside the blue tunnel that was the timestream. The golden light of the tether again shone behind her, stretching back to the gateway. Amelia turned off her valence-phaser and looked back at the window, where images of the past played in an endless loop. Now that she had completed the synchronization, the analysts would be able to study everything she'd experienced from the safety of the present.

"Reentry confirmed," Gavin said. "We'll be waiting for you on the other side."

"I'm making my way back to the gateway now," Amelia said, bounding back along the tunnel's shifting blue floor. Gravity held little influence in the timestream, where the laws of physics were bent and distorted. She followed the path laid out for her by the tether until the gateway came into view.

When she neared the end of the tether, Amelia came to a sudden stop. She looked back at the sea of windows punctuating the tunnel walls and faltered just outside the gateway. She stared so hard at the windows she was almost certain she could fall through just by looking at them.

I shouldn't, she thought, a look of longing on her face beneath the darkened visor.

Amelia hesitated and punched in a command disconnecting her communication system from those in the present. Time had no meaning inside the tunnel. She could remain in the timestream for minutes or hours, and it wouldn't make a difference. When she passed through the gateway, she would be returning to the exact moment the others were waiting for her. With her communications system disengaged, they would never know she had lingered behind a short while longer. Amelia knew this from experience; this wasn't the first occasion she had strayed from the mission parameters.

She was well aware she was violating a hundred rules, but she couldn't help herself. Amelia entered a destination in time and space into her gauntlet, and her visor targeted a window not far from the gateway. Amelia swallowed hard and made her way to the window. With a sigh, she disengaged the tether, turned on her valence-phaser, and entered the portal.

Unlike her foray into 1587 Roanoke, Amelia emerged in exactly the place and time she wanted. It was a piece of the past she knew well.

She floated inside a large bathroom, where a child ran a comb through tangles of hair, wet from a recent bath. The girl was young, not even tall enough to see herself in the mirror opposite the bathtub. The child's father helped her into her pajamas and playfully hoisted her over his shoulder, carrying her off to bed. Amelia reached after them as they headed out of the bathroom, but then held her hand at her side and followed behind.

She watched as the girl's father read her a bedtime story. His face was kind and full of laughter. His daughter looked at him with an enormous smile, like he was the most important thing in the world. When he was finished with the story, the man closed the book, leaned forward, and kissed his daughter on the forehead.

"I love you, Amelia," he said.

The child's face brightened. "I love you, Daddy Buddy," she said, using her childhood nickname for him.

"I love you, too, Dad," Amelia whispered, fully aware he couldn't hear her.

Amelia's eyes stung with tears. She rewound time and replayed the moment again, pausing it at the moment her father kissed her on the forehead. The love in her father's eyes, and the unadulterated expression of joy on Amelia's young face, touched her every time. It was the same memory she watched again and again, returning with each successive mission into the past. Using time travel technology in an unapproved fashion for personal use was strictly forbidden, but if Amelia altered nothing, and her superiors never discovered what she was doing, what was the harm?

I should go, Amelia told herself. She didn't want to stay too long in the past. It was easy to lose track of time altogether when it no longer carried meaning. With a final glance at her father, she returned through the portal and emerged into the timestream.

Amelia started back toward the gateway and stopped. She paused. Sometimes, even though those she observed in the past could neither see nor hear her, Amelia had the slightest feeling they could sense they were being watched. That was how she suddenly felt inside the tunnel—like something else was observing her.

Amelia tried to shake it off. She knew she was completely alone inside the timestream. Everything in existence aside from herself remained firmly on the other side of the gateway. And yet, the feeling did not abate. With each step she took toward the gateway, it grew stronger than ever.

Just before she crossed the threshold of the gateway, Amelia looked back at the tunnel, at the wall where she had ventured into her past. She wasn't sure why, but her eyes traveled to the opposite wall. She studied the ever-shifting waves of blue with an intent gaze.

There's nothing there, she thought to herself. *You were just imagining things.* She allowed herself to relax.

That was when she noticed it for the first time. In the otherworldly twilight that extended beyond the walls of the timestream, a large shape floated in the obscuring darkness, like a tall, narrow oval. Amelia's breath caught in her chest.

There's something out there, she thought. She squinted, trying to get a better look, but she lost track of it among the floating pockets of shadow dispersed through the gray light. Amelia looked for the shape again, but nothing was there. She was alone once again. But as she turned and passed through the gateway, she couldn't shake the feeling that she was still being watched.

CHAPTER TWO

J UST LIKE THAT, SHE WAS standing on a circular protrusion at the end of a long platform inside a massive, dome-shaped chamber. Amelia exhaled, relieved at her safe return to the present. And yet, she couldn't forget the unsettling feeling she'd experienced in the moments before passing through the gateway.

It was nothing, she told herself. *My eyes were playing tricks on me.* Nothing could exist outside time and space.

She shivered, as if her body betrayed unconscious doubts. She was cold—the kind of deep, penetrating coldness Amelia always experienced whenever she first entered the timestream. The sensation had never followed her into the present before. There was something wrong about it.

Footsteps echoed a short distance away, and Amelia looked up, startled. A small group headed down the platform to greet her. She held her arms against her chest for warmth as she waited for them, still cold. Behind her, there was no trace of the gateway; the portal always closed the moment she appeared in the present. Her eyes drifted to two metal arches attached to the left and right sides of the platform's end. Wires attached to the base of each column ran deep into the chamber's walls, where they fed off the energy produced by the fusion reactor below the platform, buried under a lake of water.

"Welcome back, Dr. Lewis," Gavin said when the group reached her. He was tall and thin with a youthful face. "Another successful mission."

"Thank you, Gavin," she said as the technicians began dismantling the EMV, piece by piece.

Gavin still wore the headset directly connecting him with Amelia's communications system. He was one of the youngest ever selected to serve as one of the agency's mission leaders. He was always friendly, though he took his responsibilities seriously. As she studied his face, Amelia thought she saw a trace of concern beneath his smile.

"Is something wrong?" she asked, suddenly worried the analysts had somehow been able to detect that she had abused the time travel technology to observe memories of her father.

Gavin rubbed the back of his neck and bit his lip. "You look uneasy," he said. "Is everything alright?"

Amelia let out an inward sigh of relief. *He was just worried about me,* she thought. And with good reason, too—she was sure she looked frightened when she emerged from the gateway.

"I'm fine," she said, forcing herself to smile. "It's just the jump. You never get used to it." She raised an arm and allowed a technician to remove one of her sleeves.

Gavin chuckled. "That's why I'm glad you're the one in the timestream, and I'm nice and safe in the present."

Amelia laughed softly, and the cold feeling lessened. Now that she was back in the present, surrounded by others, she no longer felt so isolated and alone. "I have plenty of work to do in the present as well," she said. "It'll take me weeks to review and document everything I learned about Roanoke."

Time travel actually incorporated a fraction of what Amelia did at the agency. Most of her work entailed tireless research in anticipation of a mission.

"I know the higher ups will be looking forward to your final report," Gavin said. "Word is, the director is eyeing you for the Seven Wonders project."

Amelia's heart skipped a beat. "Really?" She tried and failed to keep the excitement out of her voice.

He winked and held a finger up to his lips. "I'm not supposed to say anything yet, but she was very impressed by your work on Alexander the Great."

Amelia fought the urge to grin. Exploring and documenting the Seven Wonders of the Ancient World would be one of the biggest undertakings in the organization's history. From the Great Pyramid of Giza to the Lighthouse of Alexandria, all seven wonders had been lost over the ages. The mere existence of the Hanging Gardens of Babylon was still a hotly debated historical topic. It was Amelia's dream project. She'd submitted a request to participate almost as soon as the mission was first announced. She was aware each of her colleagues had also applied, hoping to be selected for the mission.

Amelia was one cog in a large, complex machine. There were seven other temporal historians, although the temporal enforcement division outnumbered them by a two-to-one margin. Altogether, there were less than twenty-five chrononauts currently on active duty.

Gavin gazed at his wrist com and back at Amelia. "The director will be expecting us any time now for the debriefing," he said when the technicians had finished removing her suit. "We don't want to be late."

Amelia nodded and followed Gavin down the platform toward the chamber's exit, where two armed guards stood watch. Just before they crossed the threshold, she gave one last glance at the spot where the gateway had closed, and a shiver ran down her spine. Then she hurried to catch up with Gavin, who had outpaced her. They passed the mission control room, full of rows of monitors and devices. Scientists in white coats were visible through the glass, already going over the data she had collected.

They came to an elevator, where Amelia submitted to the mandatory retinal scan necessary to gain entry.

"Identity confirmed," an automated voice said, and the doors slid open. *"Lewis, Amelia Nicole."*

"Take us to the director's office," Gavin said once they were securely inside the elevator.

The doors closed, and the elevator began its ascent. It was a steep climb; the gateway chamber from where they were coming was the facility's most restricted area, built deep under the earth. There were three such chambers in all, the only government-approved time travel devices on the planet.

"I've finally got some vacation time coming up now that the Roanoke Project is complete," Gavin said. "What about you?"

Amelia smiled. "I expect I'll spend the next month or so reviewing my findings and compiling my report."

Gavin nodded, as if having anticipated her response. It was well known Amelia was one of the most hardworking individuals in the agency. She threw herself into her work and did little else. She couldn't remember the last time she'd taken real time off, even though chrononauts were encouraged to do so after each mission.

The elevator was made of transparent, reinforced glass, allowing Amelia to see the facility in its entirety as they rose higher. It was one of the largest and most secure buildings in the capital, home to the world's most advanced technology and brightest minds. The advent of time travel had the potential to change everything about the way mankind understood the universe. There was still much the scientists didn't know about the process, and Amelia counted herself lucky to be part of the initial wave of pioneers.

The elevator came to a stop on one of the middle floors, and Amelia followed Gavin outside. She was familiar with the path to the director's office, though it was one she seldom tread. The director was a busy woman tasked with overseeing the security and functionality of one of the most restricted facilities on the planet, so each second of her time was precious. For this reason, it had always impressed Amelia that the director made sure to meet with each chrononaut immediately following a mission.

"Dr. Lewis," a voice called out behind her as they made their way through an expansive hall, and Amelia cringed. She glanced over her shoulder and saw a man approaching in a hurry. He was in his late forties, with dark curly hair and olive skin that hinted at his Mediterranean origins.

"Herostratus," she said in a neutral tone, slowing to a halt. Gavin looked at Herostratus nervously but said nothing.

"You knew my graduate thesis was on Roanoke when you took that project," he said, narrowing his eyes at her. "It should have been my project, not yours." Herostratus was another of the agency's temporal historians, but they were more rivals than colleagues.

"I took the assignment I was given," Amelia said.

"You wanted to humiliate me," Herostratus replied. "I postulated the colonists were wiped out by the natives. You undid my entire thesis."

"We really should be going," Gavin said to Amelia, shifting uncomfortably, likely uneasy at the prospect of being caught in the middle of an argument between two of the agency's most prominent historians.

Amelia paid him no attention, her focus on Herostratus. "We're temporal historians, Herostratus. We don't just theorize about facts—we uncover them. If your thesis didn't pan out, perhaps you should stop blaming me and put the focus where it belongs."

Herostratus leaned in closer, and Amelia could smell his metallic breath. "You've been riding off Alexander's coattails far too long," he said. "Stay away from the Seven Wonders Project, Dr. Lewis, or you'll regret it." Then he marched away.

"Sorry about that," Gavin said as Amelia watched Herostratus go.

"You don't have anything to apologize for," Amelia said, shaking her head. "It's his problem."

They found the director waiting in her office. "Come in," she said, motioning them inside. "Dr. Lewis," she said courteously, extending a hand.

"Director Eldrich," Amelia replied as they shook hands.

"Please, be seated," she said, and Amelia and Gavin sat opposite her desk. "You'll have to excuse me if I seem a bit distracted," Eldrich said. "There was another incident involving unauthorized time travel using a homebrew system. Fortunately, a team of our temporal enforcers were able to apprehend the man before he permanently altered the timeline." She sighed. "It used to be we'd only see one or two of these incidents in a year. Now they're becoming far more frequent."

"I could come back later if you like," Amelia offered.

Eldrich shook her head. She was a thin, serious-faced woman with only a few traces of brown remaining in her otherwise gray hair. "This won't take long," she said. "Tell me about the mission."

"Everything went as planned," Amelia said. "The mission was a success. The colonists sought shelter on Croatoan, under the protection of friendly natives. Over time they intermarried, and their story was lost to the centuries—until now."

"Good work, Dr. Lewis. Is there anything else you would like to share about the mission?" she asked, interested. "Were there any anomalies?"

Amelia hesitated. "I'm not sure," she said, thinking of her last moments in the timestream.

"There's a reason we use chrononauts to observe the past instead of sending drones to do the job," Eldrich said. "In the early days of time travel, a drone malfunctioned and was lost in the past. We followed the coordinates and recovered it in the present, buried deep under ground. If any groups had discovered it before us…" She trailed off. "Human beings have judgment and intuition machines can't mimic. If you have a concern, Dr. Lewis, I would encourage you to share it with me."

Amelia nodded, reluctant. "When I was inside the timestream, I thought I saw something unusual."

Gavin looked surprised, and the director raised an eyebrow. "What do you mean?" she asked. "When did this happen?"

Amelia bit her lip. "I was on my way back to the gateway, and I felt something strange. It was like I was being watched. I thought I caught a glimpse of something beyond the tunnel walls—an oval of some kind, floating in the shadows. It was just for a moment," she added quickly.

Eldrich smiled, a rare occurrence for the director. "Are you sure?" she asked. "The scientists have assured us many times that nothing exists outside the confines of time and space."

"I know," Amelia replied. "Have either of you ever heard of anything like this before?" She looked from Gavin to the director, waiting for an answer.

"No," Eldrich said confidently, but Gavin's eyes darted away, refusing to meet her gaze.

He knows something, she thought. *Something he's not telling me.*

"I'll have the research team take a look at your video feed and see if they can find any anomalies, though I think it's more likely your visor malfunctioned. Do you have any other concerns?"

Amelia frowned. Having the team take a closer look at her feed was exactly what she *didn't* want, since it ran the risk of revealing her unsanctioned trip into the past.

"No, Director Eldrich," she said.

"If that's all, I'd like to move on to another topic," Eldrich added. "As you know, the Roanoke Project was rather smaller in scale compared to some of our other recent missions."

"I was delighted to be selected, Director Eldrich," Amelia said. "I'm grateful to be a part of what we're doing at the agency."

"I know," Eldrich replied. "You're one of the most accomplished members of your field, and an exemplary chrononaut. I know how hard you work, Dr. Lewis. That's why I've decided to name you to the Seven Wonders Project. I've reviewed your application and believe you are most suited to the job."

Amelia's face broke out into a wide grin, all thought of the previous topic forgotten. "Thank you, director," she said. "It's an honor."

"This will be the biggest historical project in the agency's history. It will involve multiple trips into the past." Eldrich looked over her wrist com. "We'll wait until after you submit your final report on Roanoke before announcing your selection."

"I'll have it to you within the month," Amelia said, and the three stood together. After thanking Eldrich again, she turned to leave.

"And Dr. Lewis?" Eldrich called after her. "I see that it's been a long while since you took any time off. See that you do before you start work on your next assignment. I want you at your best."

Amelia arrived at the restaurant early. The dining establishment was relatively upscale, which necessitated that she wear a dress. Even after all her success, it felt strange standing inside such a place. Her family wasn't well off as a child, although Amelia never considered herself poor. True wealth was measured by things other than money. Her father taught her that.

Amelia wore a simple black dress and a single strand of pearls—she wanted to remain as low-key as possible. She didn't want to send any mixed signals. She would've eschewed the dress entirely if the setting didn't demand it. When she found her way to her table, her ex-fiancée was already waiting for her.

"Amy," he said, rising from his chair when he saw her coming.

"Collin," she said, attempting a neutral smile.

"You look beautiful," Collin said as they both settled into their seats. He grinned. "I wasn't sure you would come. I didn't think they ever let you leave work these days."

Amelia fought back the first response that came to her mind and instead took a drink of water. "I've been taking some time off," she said, setting the glass back on the table.

There was something in Collin's eyes when she said it. Was it hope? Amelia wasn't sure. "That's not like you," he said.

"I'll be going back soon," she said. "I'll be leading a new project at the agency, and I needed the time to get prepared."

Collin exhaled loudly and shook his head. "Some things never change," he said, sipping his water.

Amelia felt an involuntary twitch of anger at the slight against her working hours. It was a sore point between them, or at least it had been at one time.

"I was surprised you reached out," Amelia said a few minutes after they ordered. "I wasn't expecting it."

Collin looked away. When he returned his gaze to her, it was with an intensity that caught her off guard. "I've been thinking a lot lately about how things ended between us," he said. "I wanted to see you again. We would have been together three years last month."

Amelia sighed. "We've been down this road, Collin."

The food came, interrupting the flow of conversation. Amelia reached for her fork, less than anxious to return to the topic at hand, but Collin continued staring at her like a student trying to solve a particularly perplexing math problem. "We were going to get married, Amy. Can you honestly tell me you never think about it?"

She shook her head. "Very rarely anymore," she admitted. Her words seemed to visibly wound him, but he recovered quickly.

"Don't you ever wonder how things would have been if your work at the agency didn't come between us?"

Amelia put her fork back down and decided to engage. If this was really the conversation he wanted to have, then he would get it. "You were the one who made my work into a problem."

"I was always proud of you," Collin said. "I was never intimidated by your success. But you throw yourself completely into your work, leaving no time for anything or anyone else. You don't have any friends, you rarely go out, and you're a stranger to your family."

"Leave my family out of this," Amelia snapped.

Collin's expression softened. "I know things haven't been good between you and your sister since your brother's death. Have you tried reaching out to her?" He extended his hand and took hers in his. "I just want you to be happy, Amy."

She pulled her hand back as if he had stung her. "I am happy," she said. "I love my work."

"You're not happy—you're obsessed. You live in the past at the expense of the present, and I'm not talking about time travel. I know you idealize your childhood, but things are different now. There are real relationships in the here and now that you've neglected."

"I didn't come here to be lectured, Collin."

"Then why did you come here?"

She paused. "I think...I think I was looking for closure."

He shook his head, suggesting he didn't believe her—or perhaps he didn't want to. "I don't think that's it. I think you know I care about you, and you missed having that in the real world, not some childhood memory."

"You're not being fair," she said.

"Maybe not," he replied. "Just don't forget—if you live in the past, you might get stuck there."

CHAPTER THREE

T HE DAY AFTER HER DINNER with Collin, Amelia left the capital behind and travelled by high-speed rail to the long-term care facility where her father resided. She had plenty of time to clear her head in the relative solitude of the sparsely populated boxcar. Collin's words haunted her, more so than anything she might have glimpsed inside the timestream. He understood her too well—enough to get under her skin.

She stared outside the window as the land raced by outside. Cities and industrial outposts had long ago replaced the forests of trees she'd witnessed in 1587 Roanoke. The planet was a far different place than it once was. In many respects, that was a good thing. Science and technology had advanced to the point where most illnesses and diseases that had plagued humankind from birth were largely eradicated. Fusion reactors generated enough renewable, clean energy to power the entire planet. The climate could be controlled to maximize crop yields and limit damage from natural disasters. The overpopulation crises of the twenty-third and twenty-fourth century were a thing of the past. Perhaps most importantly, the united world government had ushered in an era of peace without war.

It was far from the dystopian portrait historical literature so often painted of the future. And yet, sometimes Amelia wondered about what had been lost in the process. Aside from international monuments and land preserves, what little land not used for cities or industry existed mainly in the form of massive farms tasked with producing the world's food supply. Entire generations would grow up thinking of things like forests or natural rivers as relics of the past. Something about that made the historian in her unfathomably sad.

She caught a glimpse of her reflection in the window and frowned. Was that a strand of gray she saw? Amelia studied her features. She had sleek, black hair, green eyes, and pale skin from long hours spent inside at her research. As she peered closer, she noticed bags under her eyes, and her frown deepened. She was still young—the youngest temporal historian by far—but time caught up with everyone eventually, even in an era where the natural life expectancy was well over one-hundred and fifty years of age.

Collin had accused her of wanting to live in the past. But what if that wasn't such a bad thing after all? What if the past was better than the present? Amelia would never grow old in the past. Her father was still healthy, and she remained close with her siblings. If she actually could re-experience the past through time travel, what was the harm in it?

A quick scan of the microchip implant in her hand to pay for a meal, and Amelia was off to see her father. Despite Collin's insistence that she had grown estranged from her family, he was wrong in at least one respect—she always made time to see her father. Amelia had picked his care facility herself, based on its proven record of excellence and proximity to the capital. It was her money that paid for his care, thanks to the hefty salary she earned as a chrononaut. Amelia would gratefully give it all up for one more day with her father as he was, but she couldn't, leaving her memories of him the next best thing.

She arrived at the long-term care facility just after midday. The building was in a tranquil location on the city's periphery, surrounded by a small grassy field and even a few trees. Amelia passed a fountain as she made her way down the walkway toward the glass doors. She looked up at the window to her father's room several floors above; Amelia had made certain he was given a room with a view.

She passed through the sliding glass doors that granted her entry. The building's interior was pristine, although that was true of every building in the modern era. A full-time staff, whose ranks included some of the best physicians and specialists available, was on hand to respond to any issues with the patients housed within the facility's walls.

After checking in and receiving an in-person update on her father's condition, Amelia thanked the physician and took the elevator to the patient wing of the facility. She stopped outside her father's room and drew in a deep breath before knocking on the door. There was no response—not that she was expecting one—but she always made sure to knock just the same. It was a show of respect.

The door opened for her mechanically, revealing the room's shadowy interior. The lights were turned off, although strands of sunlight filtered through the blinds, where a hoverchair faced the window. "Daddy?" Amelia said softly, stepping inside the quiet room.

Again there was no answer. The door slid shut behind her, leaving them alone inside the room. Amelia rounded the hoverchair and came face-to-face with her father. The man she remembered from her trip into the past was gone, replaced by the shrunken specter who now watched her from the confines of his hoverchair. Sometimes, the man in the past seemed more real than one in front of her now.

"Hello, Daddy Buddy," she said, trying to conceal the emotion in her voice. She flashed him a brilliant smile and attempted a bright affect in a hope some of it managed to get through to him. "I missed you," she added, hugging him.

Her father craned his neck and followed her nominally

with his eyes, but his expression was vacant. When he opened his mouth, the only sound that emerged was a barely-audible gurgling noise. Amelia never knew if it was in response to her or merely the random firing of damaged synapses.

Periodic beeps from a cluster of wall monitors interrupted the silence in punctuated intervals. Amelia stepped away from her father for a moment and examined the vitals and scans displayed on the monitors. She was not a physician, but all students were taught about the human body and health in great detail as part of their basic education.

Amelia let out a sigh and turned back to face her father. She knew better than to expect a change in his condition, but it was still hard to accept that the man in her memories wasn't coming back. When she was a girl, her father always had an easy smile and a twinkle in his eyes, an irrepressible light that shown through to everyone he met. He was tall and strong, with powerful but loving hands that lifted her over his shoulder as he carried her to bed, as he had in the memory she so often frequented. That man was forever lost—in the present, at any rate. The man in the hoverchair was little more than a shell. His muscles had atrophied from disuse. His skin was pale from the lack of sunlight. He was shrunken and disheveled.

"I know it's been a bit longer than usual since I came to visit last," Amelia admitted aloud, smiling warmly. "I was busy with work." Even though she'd taken time off as instructed, Amelia had used much of the time to finalize the Roanoke report and prepare for her upcoming mission. "I got the Seven Wonders Project," she said, excited, and squeezed his hand softly. "We start soon." She left unsaid that since the project was so extensive, she'd have plenty of trips into the past during which to visit him.

Releasing his hand, she walked to the window and deactivated the digital blinds, allowing more light to flow into the room. "That's better," she said with a nod. Her father's eyes followed her. Amelia didn't know how aware he was of his surroundings. The physicians told her any level of understanding he possessed would be extremely limited at best. And yet, there were times when she swore she saw flashes of recognition in his eyes— recognition and love.

Amelia was already an accomplished historian at the onset of her father's illness. She was still in training at the agency after her selection as a potential chrononaut when she learned that her father had been infected by the Rabies II virus. The Rabies II virus was even more virulent than its precursor. It worked by traveling retrograde through the peripheral nerves to the central nervous system and eventually the brain, causing multiple areas of dead tissue and hemorrhages in addition to global inflammation. The virus had first appeared in the twenty-fourth century, although it had been almost eradicated over the following centuries. Rabies II was such a rare disease that by the time it was identified in her father, it was too late to help. The enhanced healing process that had been added to the human genetic code, combined with scientific progress in the intervening centuries, was enough to keep her father alive, but the damage was already done.

"When the human brain is irreversibly injured, cells undergo a process called liquefactive necrosis," one of the physicians had explained to her. "It is a feature practically unique to the brain. Brain tissue does not form scars. Instead, it leaves behind empty lesions—think cavities, or holes." Even with all the advances of modern technology, there was nothing the physicians could do to regrow her father's neural tissue.

"I had dinner with Collin last night," she said, adjusting her father's pillow. She sat down in a chair beside his bed and shook her head. "Maybe I shouldn't have gone. I almost stayed home. I miss him I guess." She laughed. "It feels weird to say that out loud. Things didn't end well between us. You would have liked him though, Daddy. He's a good man. Sometimes I wish things had turned out differently..." She trailed off.

There was a reason Collin's words hit her so hard. Amelia knew she had retreated from the world since her father's illness. She threw herself into her work, but most of all she lived for her glimpses into the past. Collin had called her "obsessed" with the past, and she knew that probably wasn't too far from the truth. Life was better then. It was richer when she was a girl—everyone was happy, including her. If she couldn't experience that in the present, why not spend her time immersed in the past?

"The anniversary of Eric's death is coming up," she said. "I always tell myself I'll visit his grave, but somehow I never find the time."

Amelia's relationship with her siblings had begun deteriorating even before her father was hospitalized. A few years prior, she discovered her brother was making money from marketing dangerous virtual reality simulations to pay for a drug habit. Amelia confronted him about it, and though she hadn't turned him in, she cut him out of her life. Not long after, he committed suicide.

Amelia's gaze came to rest on a vase of flowers beside her father's bed. "I see Sarah's been here recently," she said. "We don't talk that much anymore. I think she blames me for what happened to Eric. Maybe I do, too." She looked to her father for the absolution he was now incapable of offering.

"We used to be so close," she said wistfully. "Do you remember how it used to be when we were little? We were inseparable."

Between her father's illness, the loss of her brother, and her estrangement with her sister, the family life she once treasured was lost to her forever in the present. But when inside the timestream, she had access to all the best parts of her life. She could listen to her father read her a bedtime story. She could watch as she played games with her sister. She could spend time with the person her brother once was.

Given the choice between the past and the present, Amelia would choose the past every time.

"Why don't we go for a walk?" she said. "It's a particularly lovely day outside, and you shouldn't be kept inside all the time."

A slight breeze washed over them as she pushed her father's hoverchair down the walkway outside the facility. His eyes swept over the serene landscape, something he would have enjoyed when he was able. Her father had always loved nature, preferring it to the metropolitan cities that predominated much of the world.

At last, the hour grew late, and Amelia turned around and began pushing her father back toward the facility. "I love you, Daddy Buddy," she said, giving him a kiss on the cheek. "I'll see you again soon," she added, already thinking of her impending mission.

The sun burned like a torch in the cloudless sky, scorching desert sands that stretched on seemingly without end. The periodic, gentle breeze did little to abate the unforgiving heat. Sweat poured off the backs of the thousands of workers assembled underneath the shadow of the towering structure rising above the earth. Even the taskmasters, who hid their faces from the sun inside their tents, were not immune from the heat's effects. Workers and slaves often passed out from heat exhaustion.

Invisible to all, Amelia watched in awe through the visor of her EMV as the Great Pyramid of Giza neared completion. She was currently visiting the year 2560 BCE, farther than she had ever before traveled into the past.

"This is incredible," she heard Gavin say over the radio. "I've never seen anything like it."

Amelia nodded, overwhelmed by the sheer spectacle. Of all the Seven Wonders of the Ancient World, the Great Pyramid of Giza had been the last to fall to the ravages of time. Upon its completion, the pyramid had stood as the tallest man-made structure in the world for almost 4,000 years.

The pyramid itself was over 146 meters tall, and the construction methods used to create such a towering structure in an age of primitive tools had been a hotly debated subject among historians for millennia. As Amelia watched the workers drag, lift, and set rocks into place, it was a mystery that had finally been solved.

"Look," she said. The workers dragged the large stones across the dessert sands on what appeared to be giant sleds with ropes attached. But Amelia's interest fell elsewhere, where a small group poured buckets of water onto the hot sands ahead of the sleds. "They're dampening the sands," she said. "Why would they do that?"

There was a lull on the other end of the com, and Amelia continued to observe the workers as she waited for a response. To her surprise, the stones slid easily over the wet sand.

"According to our physicists, moistening the sand decreases friction, greatly reducing the amount of energy required to drag the stones across the desert. The water droplets forge intermolecular bridges with the sand particles."

"It's like building a sandcastle," Amelia said, remembering a trip to the beach with her father. "They're easier to build with wet sand, because it sticks together better."

"Exactly," Gavin said from across the reaches of time and space. "Congratulations, Dr. Lewis." They had worked closely together on the project for months, and now the massive undertaking had begun in earnest.

"One down," she said. "Six to go." The pyramid was the first of the ancient wonders Amelia had visited, but the project was off to a successful start. Yet even as she tried to concentrate on the task at hand, Amelia felt distracted and anxious. She found herself counting down the seconds until she was finished with the current mission, so that she could secretly visit another of her childhood memories upon her return to the timestream.

"I think that's enough for today," she said after waiting as long as she could bear.

"Are you sure?" Gavin asked. "You've only been there a short time."

"I've learned much today," she replied. "I have a lot to document. Besides," she added, "we still have a few visits to Egypt left before we'll be ready to move on to the next wonder." She smiled under her helmet. More trips into the timestream meant more unsanctioned visits to her past.

"It's your call," Gavin said, but he didn't sound convinced.

Amelia punched in the command to renter the timestream on her gauntlet's keypad.

Tether engaged, flashed across her visor as Amelia felt herself pulled out of the past.

She crossed through the window in time and emerged inside the timestream, once more surrounded by walls of ethereal blue light interspersed with the glowing mirrors into the past. The golden tether attached to her back held her in place, disappearing as it stretched toward the gateway to the present. Amelia was too far along the tunnel to see the gateway from her current position. She was farther along the tunnel's course than ever before, and yet she seemed no closer to its end. Amelia often wondered if the timestream stretched on for eternity without an end, or if it simply went to the beginning of time as the scientists claimed.

"Reentry confirmed," Gavin said as she floated in place. "We'll be seeing you shortly."

Amelia's heart skipped a beat. A few moments longer, and she would be ready to observe her memories again. She turned off her valance-phaser and started to adjust her suit's density when a familiar cold sensation seized her in its icy grip, and once more she experienced the feeling of being watched. She looked around, searching for the source as the tunnel walls continued to rotate.

Suddenly, all the white surfaces strewn across the blue walls—the windows into the past—glowed in unison.

That's never happened before, Amelia thought.

As she looked on in horror, every single window now played the same scene over and over again. It was a memory she recognized instantly: her most recent dinner with Collin.

What's happening? she wondered, chill bumps covering her skin. Something was very wrong.

"Gavin, are you seeing this?" she asked, but static interrupted his reply.

Communications systems offline, the A.I. announced as Amelia vigorously hit the side of her helmet, trying to reengage the radio.

Without warning, all the images unfolding on the windows stopped moving, frozen on Collin. A chill ran down her spine, and she turned around on instinct and looked behind her.

Amelia found herself unable to breathe. In the gray twilight outside the tunnel's walls, a massive form hovered in the nothingness. It was the same shape she'd glimpsed before, only this time it was no longer hidden in one of the many pockets of shadow strewn across the twilight. It was a featureless oval, tall and narrow. Her watcher possessed an obsidian color, with a smooth surface that seemed to swirl inwardly like a black hole. Although the watcher had no discernable eyes, she knew it was watching her even as she gazed at it.

I need to get to the gateway, she realized. *Now.*

Amelia bounded along the path of the tunnel, but the watcher did not move. Without warning, her tether snapped. Amelia's eyes widened as the golden cord slid along the tunnel's path. Her temporal stabilizers anchored her in place inside the timestream, but without the tether, she would never be able to find her way to the gateway, and to the present. Thrown off balance, she stumbled backward and collided with the tunnel wall. She toppled over the side and felt herself falling toward the nothingness that waited outside the tunnel's walls. Amelia managed to grab hold of the path at the last moment, and she found herself dangling from the timestream.

Behind her, the watcher began inching toward her.

"Can anyone hear me?" she shouted into her radio, but there was only the static sound of interference. "I need help!"

The watcher drew even closer, and her body began to shudder. Amelia struggled fiercely to climb back onto the path, but her EMV weighed her down.

"What are you?" Amelia pleaded with the watcher. "Why are you doing this?"

Suddenly, the windows on the tunnel's walls began to glow again. This time, instead of the solitary image with Collin, each window displayed a different scene from the past—but all featured Amelia.

As the watcher drew nearer, the alien coldness grew. Her visor began to fog and her teeth chattered violently. Her legs dangled wildly over the ledge, unable to flee as the watcher continued its approach. At the last second, Amelia succeeded in pulling herself onto the path, although intense pain along the course of her arm warned her she'd probably torn a muscle in her shoulder—or worse.

She regained her footing and stumbled forward, cradling her shoulder. The watcher paused outside the walls of the timestream, and for a moment she thought she was safe. Then the watcher passed through the blue light, closing in on her.

Amelia broke into a dead sprint toward the place where the tether had landed. She lunged toward it and grabbed the end of the golden cord seconds before the watcher reached her. There was no time to reconnect the tether to its rightful place on the back of her EMV, so instead she tugged on the cord and activated the return to the gateway. It began shortening as the end passed through the distant gateway, dragging Amelia along with it. She held on desperately with her good arm, even as she was smashed wildly against the walls of the tunnel. Her suit was ripped and torn, and her exposed skin was scraped and bleeding. Just when she thought she couldn't hold on any longer, the gateway loomed a short distance away.

She saw her hand begin to vanish into the portal, still clutched around the tether. Then she lost consciousness, and everything faded to black.

CHAPTER FOUR

MELIA FOUND NO SOLACE IN her dreams from what haunted her. Images—real and imagined—flashed by in disjointed fragments. She saw herself as a girl, running to her father. She drew closer to him, and her father transformed into Collin, who in turn became the Watcher.

"If you live in the past, you might get stuck there," Collin's last words to her echoed loudly seconds before she woke.

Amelia let out a soft moan and opened her eyes. *Where am I?* she wondered. *What happened?* Everything was a blur. When she tried to focus on her memories of what had happened, she experienced a brief flash of images from the timestream, accompanied by a sharp pain in her head.

She was lying in bed inside a well-lit room. Nearly everything in the room was white, including the furniture, the paint on the walls, and the sheets on her bed. A transparent set of glass doors was the only thing she could see that wasn't white. Amelia managed to sit up. Her entire body throbbed with dull aches and pains.

I feel like I've been hit by a building, she thought, minimizing her movements to avoid undue soreness. Her eyes fell on a group of monitors displaying multiple sets of vital signs, and she realized she was inside a hospital room. When she looked down at herself, Amelia noticed she was wearing a loose-fitting hospital gown.

How did I get here? she wondered. She had no memory of passing through the gateway, or what had happened when she reached the other side. The last thing she could recall was the tether forcefully dragging her through the tunnel.

Maybe it was all a dream, she thought. The thing she had encountered inside the timestream seemed too impossible to be real, and yet the imagery of it was so vivid and unsettling.

"Hello?" she called out. "Is anyone there?" She felt cold, even though the monitors recorded her temperature as normal. She held her arms close to her chest for warmth, but it did little to dispel the troubling sensation.

She thought again of Collin's warning. How well he understood her, even after all this time. She found herself wishing she had acted differently during their dinner conversation. Whatever he'd said, it had only been because he cared about her.

She often wondered what went wrong with their relationship. After their breakup, Amelia had tried to forget about Collin, as she did with everything else, by burying herself in her work. But now, as she lay alone in the hospital bed, she looked at the empty visitor's chair and realized she missed him. They had loved each other, and it hurt to have lost that. And he wondered why she preferred to live in the past.

The glass doors slid open, and a physician entered the room. "Excellent," he said. "You're awake."

"Where am I?" she asked, struggling to move. "What happened?"

"Easy," the physician said. "You've been asleep for three days."

"Three days?" Amelia asked, shocked.

The physician nodded. "Your body has endured quite an ordeal," he said, calling up a series of images on a screen. "Your right arm was broken in three places, along with severe rotator cuff injuries. Nearly all your ribs were broken, and you had a collapsed lung, a shattered left femur, and multiple torn ligaments and tendons, in addition to multiple lacerations and abrasions."

"My God," Amelia muttered upon hearing the full extent of her injuries.

"From what I'm told, your suit probably protected you from even worse damage, but you were in serious condition when you were brought in. We were able to stabilize your vitals and begin the regenerative process."

Thanks to genetic engineering, an enhanced healing factor provided increased resistance to wounds and infections, leaving many once life-threatening injuries now survivable with the right support. Given this, it was little surprise that the human lifespan had increased so dramatically, along with other advancements in medicine and technology. Despite these advantages, Amelia still found it difficult to move, even if she knew it wouldn't take long for her body to finish healing at an accelerated pace.

"We're going to keep you here for at least one more night for observation," the physician said. "If you don't have any questions for me, some of your colleagues will be anxious to speak with you once they learn you're awake."

It wasn't long after he left that the glass doors slid open again. Gavin entered, a look of concern on his face, followed by Director Eldrich. When Gavin saw Amelia sitting up in bed, he breathed a sigh of relief and smiled at her. In contrast, Eldrich's face was an expressionless mask.

"Thank God you're all right," Gavin said, finding his way closer to her bedside. "I haven't slept a wink."

"What happened?" Amelia asked in an attempt to put the pieces together.

"That's what we were hoping you could tell us, Dr. Lewis," Eldrich said.

"The last thing I remember is passing through the gateway," Amelia said. "Everything after that is a blank."

"When you appeared in the present, you were unconscious," Gavin said. "Your EMV was tattered and covered in blood. We removed your suit and moved you here as quickly as we could."

"We've never had anything like this happen before," Eldrich

said. "Temporal enforcers have been injured in the line of duty, but never a temporal historian. And never once inside the timestream." She studied Amelia with an expression of curiosity. "What happened when you emerged from the window?"

Amelia's brow furrowed. "Couldn't you see?" she asked. "My suit…"

Gavin cut her off. "Your communications system went offline," he answered. "Something was interfering with your feed. We checked your suit's internal monitors, but the data was lost. It must have been damaged when you were dragged back to the gateway."

"That can't be," Amelia muttered, recalling the static she'd heard when she tried to radio the others. There was no proof of what she'd encountered in the tunnel. She buried her face in her hands, physically and emotionally exhausted.

Eldrich wouldn't be deterred. "I know you're tired, Dr. Lewis, but I'm going to have to ask one more time: what exactly happened inside the timestream? Without footage, we have no way of determining the events that led to your injury. We need to know so that we can ensure it doesn't happen again."

Amelia looked up and nodded, drawing on her reserves of energy. *They have to know,* she thought. "Do you remember what I told you when I completed the Roanoke mission?" she asked. "About what I thought I saw beyond the timestream's walls? There was something there." Amelia's voice grew stronger. "I saw it again. It was… watching me."

"What was watching you?" Eldrich asked skeptically.

Amelia broke eye contact. "I don't know how to describe it," she stammered, recalling the monstrous entity's monolithic appearance. "It was like nothing I've ever encountered before. It caused memories of my ex-fiancée to play on the tunnel windows. I think it was what interfered with the communications systems. When I tried to return to the gateway, the tether snapped, and

I almost fell through to the region outside the tunnel. I barely made it back to the tether in time."

The director shook her head and sighed. "It's obvious what happened," she said. "Your tether became disengaged somehow, and the trauma of being dragged through the timestream caused you to hallucinate the existence of some monstrosity. Gavin, make sure the scientists and technicians carefully analyze the tether and Dr. Lewis' EMV for causes of the malfunction."

"Yes, Director Eldrich," Gavin said, inclining his head.

Eldrich laid a hand on Amelia's shoulder. "You're going to be fine," she said. "It's perfectly natural to be disoriented after going through such an ordeal."

I know what I saw, Amelia thought defiantly, but she remained quiet. It was clear Eldrich would never believe without evidence that something could exist outside time and space. Instead, Amelia looked to Gavin. He again refused to meet her gaze.

"What about the Seven Wonders Project?" she asked, returning her attention to the director.

"Further missions will be postponed until your complete recovery, as long as you're still up to the task. In the interim, Herostratus will be supervising the project. He'll be going over your findings until you're back on your feet."

Herostratus, Amelia thought. How convenient for him that she had been attacked, and now her rival was temporarily heading the project he had so desperately wanted. Something about that struck her as suspicious. Amelia's head started throbbing, and she massaged her temples. If only she could think clearly. Eldrich was right about one thing—she did need rest.

"I think I may need to take a few days' leave," Amelia said.

"Of course," Eldrich said. "The project will still be there when you return. You're very brave, Dr. Lewis," she added. "Chrononauts like you are the reason this agency exists."

As they left her in the hospital room, Amelia's eyes narrowed in Gavin's direction. Even more so than before, she was certain there was something he was keeping to himself.

What does he know? she wondered. She fell asleep without any answers.

She was released from the hospital the next day. Physically, she felt fine. Her injuries had vanished and she was clearheaded again, but Amelia knew it would be a long while before she fully recovered from her ordeal in the timestream. Beyond the emotional turmoil, a small remainder of the foreign coldness continued to follow her. It seemed to permeate her very being, as if to let her know everything was not all right.

Her first night home she barely slept. The next day she woke in the middle of the afternoon, which was unsettling to someone who normally rose early. She tried losing herself in work, but she found herself distracted, frequently flashing back to what had occurred during her mission.

How easy it would have been to blame everything on a hallucination induced by her injuries, as Director Eldrich suggested. As far as Amelia knew, there was nothing in the scientific literature hinting something like the Watcher could exist. Where would a being like that even come from? What did it want with her?

She debated whether to go back to the project at all. If she returned to the timestream, would the Watcher be waiting for her—or would it target the next chrononaut to pass through the gateway? Maybe then the agency would realize something was wrong. Amelia thought about trying to persuade Eldrich to look into the matter further, but it seemed fruitless. The director's mind was made up.

Worst of all, Amelia still had the distinct impression that she was being observed, even in the safety of the present.

I need help, she admitted to herself. She wanted someone she could talk to without fear of reprisal—someone who would listen honestly and sympathetically. More than that, Amelia needed a friend to be there for her.

No names came to mind. There was a time when she would have turned to her father, but those days were long gone, stolen by his illness. Her brother was dead, and she and her sister no longer spoke. She couldn't talk about what she'd experienced with anyone from the agency, not that she had any friends there. It was a sobering thought to realize perhaps what Collin said was true. She had buried herself in her work and in her memories, choosing the easy comforts of past at the expense of life in the present. Now, when she needed a friend, she had no one to turn to.

There is someone *I could call,* she thought, retrieving her ex-fiancée's contact information. Despite everything that had happened between them, she and Collin still cared about each other. She trusted him implicitly.

To her surprise, there was no record of Collin's contact information in her primary communications system. *That's odd,* Amelia thought. *I don't remember deleting it.* She checked again, but it was nowhere to be found. She sighed and instead turned to her personal database, where she still kept a file containing records from their time together.

When Amelia's eyes settled on the results of her search, her heart skipped a beat.

"That's impossible," she whispered aloud. There was no folder matching that description. Her pulse racing, she began searching for the files individually. There was nothing. Photographs, letters, contact information—everything had been erased. No physical or digital copies remained.

She suddenly thought of the images of their dinner playing on the tunnel walls in the moments before the tether snapped.

Don't panic, she told herself. *There has to be an explanation for this.*

A thorough search revealed that none of the physical keepsakes from their relationship remained in her living space. They too had been removed. Amelia shook her head, trying to process what was happening. If for some reason Collin had decided to collect these things, wouldn't she have remembered it? A nagging thought echoed in the corner of her mind, a haunting suspicion she couldn't yet give voice to.

I'll just have to find him another way, she thought. Amelia contacted Collin's workplace, only to discover that they had no record of his employment.

"That can't be," she said. "He's been with you for ten years."

"I'm sorry," replied the voice on the other end of the line. "I checked the records twice. No one by that name has worked here in the last fifteen years."

Amelia started to despair when another approach occurred to her, and she searched for information for Collin's parents. To her relief, she located their information in a public database.

"Hello," she said when she heard Collin's mother's voice on the other end of the line. "It's Amelia. I'm sorry to bother you, but…"

"Amelia?" The woman sounded confused. "Do we know each other?"

Amelia was stunned. "I was your son's fiancée," she stammered. "Surely you remember me."

"I think you have the wrong person," Collin's mother said politely. "My husband and I never had children." With that, she terminated the connection, leaving Amelia grappling with the news.

That's not possible, she thought. In the hours that followed, she tried everything—including a government source—in an attempt to find a record of Collin. There was no evidence of Collin in any database or record in the public domain.

How can this be happening? she wondered. It was almost as if he'd never existed at all. Amelia trembled with sudden realization. Collin had been erased from history. Someone had altered the past so that he was never born, and now she was the only one who remembered him. She fought back tears. Everything they had shared—all their memories—it was as if they had never happened. For all intents and purposes, they never had.

I must be immune because I was in the timestream, Amelia thought. *Whoever is doing this wants me to know what's happening.* It was too much of a coincidence to overlook. She was a time traveler, and now her ex-fiancée had been wiped from existence. She thought again of her encounter with the Watcher.

Usually if something in the past was altered, the agency would be aware and would take steps correct the alteration to the timeline. Whoever had altered history had somehow managed to avoid alerting the temporal enforcers, which was impossible— unless they knew the way the system operated from the inside.

"Herostratus," she muttered.

His words to her were still clear in her mind. "Stay away from the Seven Wonders Project, Dr. Lewis, or you'll regret it," he had told her.

Amelia's hand balled into a tight fist, and she wiped away her tears.

When she saw him, Herostratus was sitting in *her* chair, talking to *her* team about *her* project. Amelia waited until the meeting was over and everyone had begun filing outside the room before she confronted him. Several people looked at her with surprise as she passed. No doubt they hadn't expected her to return to work so quickly. But Amelia hadn't come to work.

Herostratus didn't notice her enter the room. He was busy going through data and notes on several screens embedded into the surface of the conference table. The sight of him caused her heart to burn with rage, and she swept toward him, causing him to finally look up and take note.

"Dr. Lewis?" he asked, his brow furrowed with confusion.

Amelia was having none of it. She grabbed him and slammed him against the wall, pinning her forearm against his throat.

"Did you really think I'd let you get away with it?" she demanded, narrowing her eyes. "How did you do it? Did you use some kind of drone to watch me while I was inside the timestream? Is that what that thing is?" She eased off his throat to allow him to speak.

"I don't know what you're talking about," Herostratus answered, coughing. The arrogance that usually graced his face was gone, replaced by fear.

"You're lying," Amelia said. "What did you do to Collin?"

"Who? I don't understand," he pleaded. There was no recognition in his eyes when she said the name.

He's telling the truth, she realized.

"Amelia?" Gavin's voice asked, full of shock, and she saw him standing in the doorway. "What's going on?"

She loosened her hold on Herostratus, who gingerly caressed his throat before hurrying out of the room.

"Rest assured, Lewis, Dr. Eldrich will be hearing about this!" he shouted on his way out.

Gavin hurried over to her side. "What was that about?" he asked, concerned. "Are you all right?"

Amelia shook her head sadly. "I don't know," she muttered. "Something's wrong."

Gavin laid a hand on her shoulder. "You're going to be okay," he said. "You're still shaken up from the accident. What are you even doing here?"

"You don't understand," Amelia said. "Something's happening to me. I'm being haunted by something I saw inside the timestream." She met his eyes. "When I told Eldrich what I saw in the timestream, both times you looked away. You know something, Gavin."

"You heard the director," Gavin answered almost reflexively. He looked uncomfortable. "Nothing that exists outside the timestream has ever been documented." He turned to go.

"Please," Amelia said, grabbing his arm. "I know what I saw. I need to know what it is. Tell me what you know."

Gavin sighed. "I don't know much," he said. "But you're not the first person to report encountering something unusual outside the timestream."

Amelia almost gasped. "There are others?"

"Only one." He shook his head. "I shouldn't be telling you this. The case files were sealed."

"Please," she asked again.

Gavin looked around, as if to make sure they were alone, and shut the door. "I'm only telling you this because I care about you." He stared down at the floor for a moment before continuing. "Five years ago, there was another chrononaut who claimed to have encountered some kind of entity during a mission. He had grown unhinged. He believed the entity was removing people from his life—erasing them from existence."

All the hair on the back of her neck stood on end. "What happened?" she asked.

"The agency conducted a thorough investigation, but there was no evidence to support his claims. His mental state deteriorated, and he was involuntarily committed to a long-term psychiatric facility for his own safety. He's been there ever since."

"Tell me his name," she said.

CHAPTER FIVE

HISTORY PAINTED A HORRIFIC PICTURE of the asylums of the nineteenth and twentieth centuries. Those dubbed insane were often imprisoned against their will and subjected to brutal experimental treatments—or the cruel neglect of indifference. Starved and locked away from the outside world in dark, cramped conditions, few patients ever recovered. Instead, these institutions bred further insanity.

Although conditions had improved dramatically over the centuries, this was always the picture Amelia held in the back of her mind. The care facilities were cleaner, the treatment more humane, but something unsettling lurked behind the sterilized veneer presented to the outside world. Despite centuries of advances in medicine, mental illness was something that simply could not be eradicated.

As Amelia walked down a well-lit hallway, accompanied by a psychiatrist and an orderly, she couldn't help thinking about the gothic appearance of the asylums she'd studied as a student.

"Mr. Wells receives so few visitors," the psychiatrist said matter-of-factly. "In fact, there's no record of the last time anyone came to talk to him since he was institutionalized five years ago."

"What about family or friends?" Amelia asked.

The psychiatrist shook his head. "We tried contacting those who knew him in hopes of understanding his frame of mind, but he has no known family or friends." Something in the man's voice was sad. "I think your visit will do him good, to be honest."

"Do you think he's dangerous?" Amelia questioned.

The psychiatrist shook his head. "No," he said. "Despite his delusions, he's quite harmless. He poses no threat to you or anyone else. But I'm not sure he would choose to leave even if it were an option."

"What do you mean?" she asked.

They came to stop outside a set of doors to a large room. The psychiatrist removed a keycard from his coat and held it in his hand. "Mr. Wells prefers to be alone," he said. "He never ventures outside his room. Most of his time is spent with his books and drawings." Before Amelia could ask any further questions, the psychiatrist slid the keycard across a sensor on the door, unlocking it.

Access granted, a message flashed on the sensor.

"I'll leave you to it then," the psychiatrist said. He nodded to the orderly. "Eric will remain here to ensure your safety."

"Thank you," Amelia said. "I appreciate the speed of your cooperation on such short notice."

The psychiatrist smiled. "For a chrononaut? Think nothing of it." And with a polite nod, he turned and walked down the hallway the way they had come, leaving her alone with the orderly.

Amelia sighed and held her palm against the glass surface of the door, and it slid open. The orderly waited behind her as she stepped across the threshold. It was dark inside the chamber. Unlike her father's room, there were no windows to allow sunlight to filter inside. Instead, the only illumination came from several dim overhead lights, creating a shadowy interior.

She noticed the drawings first. They were everywhere, scores of paintings and sketches alike plastered all over the walls. Most of them were done in pencil by violent, sweeping motions. Nearly all of them featured the same subject: a narrow oval with an obsidian surface like a black hole, which Amelia recognized as the Watcher. Her eyes widened in recognition.

Amelia approached one of the walls for a closer inspection of the sketches. Other drawings featured chrononauts inside the timestream. But the ones that held her gaze the longest were the portraits—simple renderings of different people Amelia did not recognize. The same faces appeared again and again, as if the artist hadn't wanted to forget them.

"I don't believe we've met," a voice said, startling her.

Amelia looked up and saw a man sitting at a desk beside a digital bookshelf. "Agent Wells? I'm Dr. Lewis." She approached the spot where he was seated.

Wells was busy at work on another drawing and did not look up to acknowledge her. "I'm not in the mood to talk to another psychiatrist today," he said.

"I'm not that type of doctor," she said. "I'm a temporal historian—a chrononaut, like you."

The pencil fell out of his hand, and Wells looked up instantly. His eyes bore into her with a frightening intensity, but his expression was not threatening. Instead he wore a look of resignation, sadness even.

"You've seen it," he said. Amelia thought she heard empathy in his voice.

She felt herself stiffen at the words. "How can you tell?"

"The coldness you carry with you," he answered. "Please, have a seat." He gestured to a chair close to his desk.

"Your drawings are very good," she said, looking at the walls.

Wells laughed. "I've had a lot of time to practice," he said.

"Agent Wells, I need to know what's happening to me," she said, hoping against hope he held the answers she was seeking.

"That's simple enough," Wells said. "You are being haunted."

Amelia raised an eyebrow. "What do you mean?"

Wells sighed. "I can tell you what you want to know, but the answers probably won't make much of a difference."

"Please," Amelia said. "You're the only person who can help. Everyone else thinks I'm…" She trailed off.

"Crazy?" he finished for her. "If only," he muttered. He studied her carefully in the dim light. "Has it taken anyone from you yet?"

Amelia nodded slowly. "My fiancée," she said. "There's no record of him anywhere. None of his friends or family have ever heard of him. It's as if he never existed."

"He never did," Wells said. "It erased him from the timeline."

"How do you know all this?" she asked.

Wells hesitated before answering, as if collecting his thoughts. "Five years ago, I was a temporal enforcer," he said. "I was one of the best. My partner and I stopped over a dozen illegal time travelers from permanently altering the prime timeline." He pointed to a portrait on the wall set apart from the others, one of the few done in color. Amelia followed his gaze to the portrait of a red haired woman with freckles and a fair complexion. "Her name was Rebecca," he said softly. His voice shook. "I loved her, but I never told her."

"What happened?" Amelia asked.

Wells glanced away from the picture, as if he couldn't bear to look at it for any prolonged length of time. "On one of our missions, Rebecca saw something outside the tunnel walls. I told her she was mistaken, but she kept seeing it every time we entered the timestream. Then I started seeing it too."

"The Watcher," Amelia said.

Wells inclined his head in affirmation. "We tried to convince our colleagues in the agency, but no one believed us."

Amelia leaned forward, a lump in her throat, and asked her most pressing question. "What is it?" she asked. "The Watcher, I mean."

Wells shrugged. "I've spent the last five years trying to answer that question, and I still don't know myself."

"You must have some idea."

Wells looked away from her and stared at one of the largest pictures of the Watcher sketched on the wall. "They're entities that are not limited by the restraints of space and time," he said.

"They can travel through time without being seen and manipulate events as they see fit."

"They?" she asked.

"I believe there are others beyond the one you encountered," he said. "How many, I'm not sure. They all appear the same physically." He motioned to the digital bookshelf. "Ancient scriptures refer to creatures known as the Nephilim—the Watchers." The word sent a tingle down the base of her neck. "Supernatural entities unbound by the laws of nature."

"Are you sure?" Amelia asked skeptically.

Wells raised his hands, as if to indicate the matter was pointless. "Whatever they really are, I tend to think of them as guardians of the timestream, carefully watching to make sure no one tampers with time."

"Chronoauts don't alter time," she protested.

"No, but we're the only ones who venture inside the timestream. Think about how eagerly mankind delved into the past, never thinking about what else might exist beyond the edges of our understanding. It's our history as a species, Dr. Lewis. As a historian, that's something you should understand better than most."

"There are dozens of chrononauts," Amelia said. "Why has it targeted me?"

Wells shook his head. "I'm afraid I can't tell you that," he said. "You've drawn its gaze, Dr. Lewis, and it will never let you go."

"What do you mean?" she asked, her skin covered with chill bumps.

"When Rebecca and I returned to the timestream, we knew it would be waiting for us. She thought we could stop it, but she was wrong. It came for me, and she gave herself up so that I could escape back through the gateway. I watched her disappear outside the tunnel walls." His voice broke. "When I returned to the present, there was no record of Rebecca's existence. She had been erased. I tried to explain what had happened, but everyone thought I was crazy. That's how I ended up here," he said, gesturing to the confines of the room. "Do you understand now? The Watcher won't stop with your fiancée. He was only the beginning. This entity will erase everyone you've ever known or cared about—all the people most precious to you—one by one, until it gets what it wants."

"And what is that?" she asked, dreading the answer.

"You," he answered. "It wants to take you to the ether where it resides, outside time and space, into nothingness forever. Like it did to Rebecca. Like it wanted to do to me."

The idea was too terrible to imagine. "What can I do?"

Wells looked away. "Don't go back," he said. "For some reason, it can't touch us in the present—only the people we care about. I think it's because spending time inside the timestream affords us some kind of protection. That's why the Watcher is targeting those close to you. It's trying to lure you back to the timestream, so it can take you." He offered a weak smile. "But if you stay in the present, you'll be safe."

Her eyes narrowed. "What will happen to those I love?"

Wells exhaled slowly. "They'll all be erased," he said. "It will be as if they'd never been born. Only you will know differently." He looked at the faces of the portraits on the wall, and she could see tears in his eyes. "Eventually, you'll start to forget them yourself."

Amelia thought of Collin and then of her father and sister. "I won't stand by and watch the people I love suffer a fate worse than death. Please, there has to be a way to stop it."

Wells shook his head. "There's nothing you can do," he answered. "You can only try to survive."

Amelia hardly slept that night. Finally, she gave up trying. Although she couldn't see the Watcher, she knew it was out there somewhere, beyond the limits of time and space. She could feel it. They were connected somehow. Even now it was watching her—waiting for her.

Wells' words haunted her. He had chosen life at the expense of seeing everyone he ever knew slowly removed from existence. Did that make him a coward? Amelia couldn't bring herself to pass judgment on him. The mere thought of her own near-fatal encounter with the Watcher inside the timestream was enough to make the hair on her arms stand on end. The prospect of returning to the timestream terrified her.

She wondered if there were other chrononauts besides Wells and his partner who had suffered the same fate. If there were, no one would ever know. Once they were taken beyond the timestream's walls, they too would be lost forever. She was up against something of which she had no understanding, an entity of incalculable power.

Maybe Wells was right, she thought. *Maybe it's pointless to try.*

Then she thought of Collin and all the memories they'd shared—memories of events that had now never happened. She thought of her father and sister, who were also in danger.

I'm sorry, she thought. *It's my fault. I did this to you.*

Wells claimed to have no understanding of what had drawn the Watcher's gaze, but in her heart, Amelia knew. If the watchers were indeed guardians of the timestream, Amelia's unauthorized use of time travel for personal reasons might have alerted it to her presence. While it was true she hadn't altered the past, she had abused the timestream for her own desires. And now everyone she still cared about was in danger because of her.

In the morning, she contacted her sister. It had been years since they had spoken.

"Sarah?"

"Is there something I can do for you, Amy? Is this about Dad?" The stiff tone in her sister's voice pained Amelia.

"No," Amelia said. "It's nothing like that." There was a pause as Amelia searched for the right words. "I wanted to say I'm sorry. I'm sorry for not being there. I'm sorry for Eric. I'm sorry for everything." She battled back the tears, and her voice broke. "I didn't know… I never wanted any of this to happen."

"Is something wrong?" her sister asked. The indifference in her voice was like a dagger in Amelia's heart.

She had planned to tell Sarah she was in danger, but Amelia realized that even if Sarah believed her, it wouldn't make a difference. Telling her about the Watcher would only frighten her.

"I…" she trailed off, unsure of what to say.

"Listen, Amy, I'm very busy at the moment. To be honest, I'm not sure if I'm prepared to have this conversation right now."

"Wait," Amelia pleaded. She wanted to beg, to grovel for her sister's forgiveness, to do and say all the things she had been afraid or unwilling to do before. "There's something I have to do," she said. "And I don't know if I'll be able to come back from it." She let out a sigh. "I want you to know how much I love you, Sarah. I know how badly I've let you down. No matter how hard it is, I promise you I'll do my best to make up for the time we've lost. I won't give up."

When the all-too brief conversation came to a close, Amelia finally allowed herself to cry for the first time since her ordeal began. She cried for what had been and for what she had lost. When she was finished, she wiped her eyes, summoned her courage for what would come next, and shed no more tears.

There was one more goodbye left to say. Amelia took the high-speed rail to her father's long-term care facility, as she had so many times before, fully aware it might very well be her last such trip. She found him awake when she arrived. She sat there with him for a long time in silence, unsure of how to start. Then she told him everything, starting from the beginning.

"I'd give anything if I could just make it like it was," she said. "Why couldn't life have stayed the same forever?" Then there would have been no need for her to return to the past. She paused. "Talking to Sarah, I think I understand now what Collin was trying to tell me." Amelia looked away from him and stared at the ground. "So much time wasted," she muttered. "When there were people who needed me right here all along. I wish I could have seen that before now."

The present was hard. There were no guarantees her decisions would end well. But it was real, good and bad alike, and it had taken the danger of losing it to make her see that. It was the beauty and tragedy of time. The past was always fixed in place, unchangeable. But the present could still be changed, even if it demanded great sacrifice.

"I don't know what's going to happen when I return to the timestream," she told him. "Whatever the Watcher is, it's unlike anything we know. But I swear to you, I'm going to try my best to stop it. I won't let it hurt you, Daddy. Not any of you."

And then what happened surprised her more than anything she had witnessed over the preceding days. Her father opened his mouth and spoke. The words were garbled, barely audible, and were gone in an instant, but she understood their meaning all the same.

"I love you," he had said.

Amelia knew it was impossible. She knew he was practically a vegetable. She understood his condition was irreversible. And yet for a moment, when she looked at her father she saw not the man he was, but who he had been—and she realized they were one and the same.

She hugged him so tightly she worried she might hurt him and kissed him on the forehead. "I love you, Daddy Buddy," she said, wishing they could remain there forever.

To continue the story, turn to the next page.
To read the original, darker ending, flip to the Alternate Ending.

CHAPTER SIX

S HE ALWAYS MADE THE WALK alone.
Amelia waited as the elevator began its descent, secure
in her EMV. She carried her helmet in her hands. She
breathed in and out calmly, her pulse steady. As the elevator
plunged toward the facility's depths, she felt the seconds ticking
away one by one.

Caution, an automated voice said when the elevator came to
a stop. *You are entering a restricted area.*

The doors opened, and Amelia walked down a solitary
hallway toward the entrance to the gateway chamber. She heard
Gavin say something over her receiver, but it hardly registered.
Her focus was on the task at hand.

She stopped briefly outside the entrance, where two guards
stood watch. Amelia submitted to a retinal scan, and somewhere
Gavin entered a complementary sequence to open the
impenetrable doors. Amelia passed between the guards without
a word and stepped over the threshold into the massive dome-
shaped chamber. When the doors shut behind her, she lowered
the helmet over her head and fastened it into place. She didn't
look back.

Amelia's footsteps echoed softly off the walls of the quiet
chamber. She advanced toward the platform at the heart of
the chamber, which had already started to glow from the light
gathering across the metallic archway. The gateway chamber
hummed with a silent energy from the fusion reactor buried

under the waters below. The energy coursed through the walls into the archway at the end of the platform.

Before Amelia reached the end of the walkway, she retrieved the tether, slid it into position in the back of her suit, and locked it in place. As she continued her approach, the golden cord also began to ebb with light.

"Gateway commencement in five," a random technician's voice echoed through the chamber. "Four."

This is it, Amelia thought. There was no turning back now—at least not for her.

"Three."

As the technician's voice continued the countdown, Amelia thought not of herself, but of those she loved. Her clenched fists shook not with fear, but with resolve. Her face glowed with an expression of determination in the gathering illumination.

"Two."

One by one, the features of her suit were highlighted as the EMV ran a pre-jump test for functionality.

Tether engaged. Temporal stabilizers activated. Valence-phaser ready. A.I. and communications systems are online.

"One."

A vortex opened under the archway, growing in size until it covered half the platform. Generated currents swept across the chamber, howling off the walls like vengeful spirits. The room darkened as most of the light was absorbed by the vortex, save for the tether's golden illumination. Amelia stood facing the portal—black surrounded by a cone of overpowering light—and bowed her head.

"Dr. Lewis, you are cleared to enter the timestream," Gavin's voice sounded in her helmet.

She stared up at the gateway, nodded firmly, and jumped into the vortex.

The sensation was always the same—the brief interlude of

overpowering white light, followed by the utter loneliness of the abyss in the moments before she emerged on the other side of the portal.

After saying goodbye to her father, she'd tried her best to come up with a way to defeat the Watcher. Every idea seemed more futile than the last, and if Wells' story was anything to go on, she didn't have that much time until the entity began removing more people from her life. So she decided to give the Watcher what it wanted: her. Either she would defeat it, and in doing so save her family, or it would erase her as Wells foretold, in which case it would no longer need to wipe her loved ones from existence. One way or another, it would end today.

Amelia had returned to work after what felt like an appropriate length of time to recover from her previous encounter with the Watcher. She was careful to avoid arousing suspicion about her motives, and as such had apologized both to Director Eldrich and Gavin for what she claimed to have witnessed, attributing the Watcher to an injury-induced hallucination. That seemed to satisfy both of them, although smoothing things over with Eldrich about her attack on Herostratus proved more difficult. Amelia used the stress over her ordeal to her advantage and offered Herostratus a place on the team, which finally cleared the way for her return to active duty. After that, it was all a matter of preparing for her next journey into the past and readying herself to face what lay ahead.

If I make it through this, she promised herself, *things are going to be different.* Amelia was finished living in the past. She realized now how much she wanted to live, and how much she still had to live for.

Amelia passed through the vortex, the tether's golden light glowing behind her. On the other side, she hovered just outside the gateway, watching the timestream's otherworldly blue light through her visor.

"Temporal flux stabilized," Gavin's voice echoed over her receiver. "Dr. Lewis, do you copy?"

Amelia didn't answer. She landed on the tunnel floor and gazed across the vast expanse of the timestream. The tunnel appeared much as it always had; the blue light pulsed under her feet with each step she took, and the white windows interspersed across the walls glowed rhythmically, like mirrors struck by a snowstorm. She looked from side to side, searching for something out of place. The timestream was empty, but Amelia knew she wasn't alone.

"Dr. Lewis?" Gavin repeated. "Amelia? Do you copy?"

Again she remained silent. She peered past the tunnel walls at the gray twilight beyond.

"I know you're there," she said. "Show yourself."

Suddenly, a deep, penetrating cold spread through the timestream, and Amelia's body shivered involuntarily. The images displayed by her visor began to twist and distort.

"Amelia?" Gavin asked, and his words grew disjointed as static enveloped the receiver. "We're having trouble establishing a visual connection. What's happening?"

"Tell my father and sister I love them," Amelia said before the transmission cut out, unsure if he'd heard her. Then she turned off the communications system, and the sound of static was replaced by the silence of the timestream.

Without warning, the Watcher descended through the roof of the tunnel. Amelia, who had been expecting it to attack from either side, was caught off guard. She stumbled back and landed on the floor. The monolithic watcher took up almost the entire height of the tunnel. It stopped, hovering in place above her, and Amelia used the opportunity to quickly push herself to her feet. She faced the creature with defiance in her heart.

"Leave my family out of this," she said. "This is between you and me."

The Watcher didn't respond. She didn't even know if it could speak, or if it was capable of speech. Instead, the windows into the past all glowed at once, and to Amelia's horror began playing images of her brother's life. She saw him as an infant, a young boy, and an adult as the moments of his life played out before her eyes, each window in an endless loop.

When she looked back, the entity had vanished from the timestream. Amelia took a step back, glancing from side to side. She fought the urge to panic. Where had it gone?

She caught a glimpse of something outside the tunnel's walls, and Amelia remembered that the Watcher existed beyond time and space.

As long as it's out there, I can't hurt it, she thought, searching for where it was hiding—if it was even hiding at all. Then she spotted it, watching her from the gray ether. Amelia approached the blue wall slowly, careful to avoid getting too close to the edge.

"What are you playing at?" she demanded.

Suddenly, the Watcher vanished again, this time reappearing behind her. Amelia spun around, but it was too late. The Watcher collided with her, and she felt herself lifted off the ground. She crashed hard against the tunnel floor as images of her brother continued to stream on the walls.

Amelia stumbled to her feet, shaken by the impact. With nothing holding it in place, the Watcher was almost impossible to pin down. In contrast, she was exposed and vulnerable to attack. She felt a sudden burst of coldness behind her, and again she was lifted off her feet. This time she was thrown against the tunnel's roof. Before she hit the floor, she was hurled backward, partially shattering her visor.

The Watcher hit her again and again, battering her and keeping her off step.

"EMV integrity compromised," her suit's A.I. announced, and

the next time she was struck, Amelia felt the primary temporal stabilizer on her chest break when she landed facedown.

Oh no, she thought. Her twin stabilizers were the only things anchoring her in a specific place in time.

"Warning," the A.I. said. *"Temporal destabilization imminent."*

Amelia saw the Watcher floating toward her, and rather than trying to back away, she lunged toward it. There was a pulse of electricity from her damaged stabilizer, and one of the white windows opened up and swallowed her whole.

Amelia felt herself falling through time. She concentrated and started to type coordinates into her gauntlet, but the Watcher appeared behind her, following her through time. Before she could react, she was standing in an open field as primitive-looking humans on overlooking hills converged toward her, casting spears and firing arrows in her direction. Amelia tried turning on her valance-phaser, but it wouldn't respond. She fled through the field, weighed down by the EMV.

Another hole in time opened up, and Amelia was suddenly standing at the base of an active volcano. Dinosaurs killed and ate each other upon the desolate rock, and she battled to stay upright as violent tremors ripped through the blackened earth. One of the raptors spotted Amelia and began chasing her, its jaws open in hungry anticipation. She finally managed to turn on the valance-phaser moments before it reached her.

Then she disappeared again. She felt herself sinking in the unfathomable depths of the ocean, surrounded by darkness everywhere. The Watcher was nowhere to be seen.

Why didn't it follow me? Amelia thought. Her mind flashed back to the images playing on the tunnel walls, and she knew why. It was going after her brother.

Amelia punched in a set of coordinates to her gauntlet to a date she had never forgotten—the day of her brother's suicide.

Please, let this work, she thought desperately. The remaining temporal stabilizer on her wrist kicked in, and she felt herself pulled through time and space one more time.

She was standing inside a room she recognized as her brother's, and there he was. Amelia was overcome. She had always avoided returning to her memories of him as an adult, and that day of all days in particular. Amelia reached toward him, but he didn't notice her, and she remembered she was invisible to him.

There was always a moment in time someone wanted to change. Time travelers were no different. So many times before Amelia had wished she could go back and prevent her father from contracting his illness or her brother from having killed himself. Although she was a chrononaut, she was still a human being. But Amelia understood why the use of time travel to alter the past was restricted. If everyone tried to go back, the timeline would be irreversibly damaged, perhaps broken altogether.

And yet, as she watched her brother, Amelia knew she had to do something. *I won't let it take him,* she thought. She knew the rules. She understood what would happen if she tried to alter the past, but she no longer cared.

"Eric?" she said, turning off the valence-phaser.

Her brother jumped, shocked by her sudden appearance. "Amy?" he asked, bewildered.

For a moment, Amelia forgot about the Watcher, the threat to her family—all of it. The only thing that mattered was that she was with her brother again. She felt hope stir inside her. Amelia felt a lump forming in her throat. How many times had she wished for this—for one last chance to say goodbye? A chance to make things right.

"Eric," she said again, reaching toward him.

There was a flash of light behind her brother as someone wearing a gold EMV appeared inside the room. As Amelia's eyes widened in shock and realization, more chrononauts began appearing inside the confines of the room, surrounding them in a circle.

Amelia started to move closer to her brother, but the first chrononaut to appear held a plasma gun trained on her.

"Don't move," said the temporal enforcer, his voice distorted by the gold helmet. The other chrononauts each aimed their plasma guns at Amelia and her brother.

"What's happening?" Eric demanded, visibly bewildered.

The temporal enforcer ignored him. "Dr. Amelia Lewis," he declared. "You are under arrest for attempting to alter the course of history."

CHAPTER SEVEN

THE VORTEX CLOSED BEHIND THEM as a final gust of wind blew across the platform. The gateway chamber fell quiet, humming with hidden power.

"You have to listen to me," Amelia said, her hands bound behind her by a set of electro-magnetic handcuffs. Two chrononauts flanked her on either side, restraining her. "We have to go back."

"Save it," ordered the lead temporal enforcer, his face still obscured by his helmet.

"Please," she said, struggling against the chrononauts holding her in place. "My family is in danger."

The temporal enforcers prodded her forward along the platform. One of them was carrying her helmet. Amelia could see her reflection in its cracked visor, broken into many parts like the windows covering the walls of the timesteam.

Suddenly the entrance to the gateway chamber opened, and Gavin hurried through, accompanied by the guards. The shock on his face was palpable.

"You tried to change the past," he said, as if he was having difficulty believing it. "You know what they're going to do to you." He shook his head, clearly concerned for her. "Why?" he asked.

"You know why," she answered, meeting his gaze before the guards ushered her outside the gateway chamber. "I demand to speak with my representative," she said as they led her away.

***

The asylum hummed with excitement. Something had happened—something big by the sound of it.

Most of the time, Wells was willfully ignorant of what went on the in the world outside the walls of his confinement. That world no longer held anything for him, not since Rebecca's death. No matter whom he loved, anyone he cared for would always end up erased by the Watcher.

For years Wells had remained in the asylum, rarely leaving his room. He feared drawing the Watcher's gaze, even years later. Time held no meaning to the entity. He took what solace he could from his books and drawings.

Then Dr. Amelia Lewis had entered his sheltered world and made him remember what he was before his encounter with the Watcher had turned him into a coward. He spent almost an entire day staring at the portrait he had drawn of Rebecca, and fear and shame yielded to an overwhelming sense of anger.

How could she go back? he wondered, unable to keep the thought from his mind. Amelia was willing to risk the almost certain possibility of being erased from existence to save her family. He remembered what it was to feel that strongly about something.

As Wells wondered what had happened to Amelia, he began to notice increased activity outside his room. When his psychiatrist came to visit him and asked him questions almost exclusively about what he had discussed with his 'visitor,' the former temporal enforcer realized something unusual was going on. He lingered at the door to his room when the psychiatrist left, listening for information.

"What did you learn?" a voice asked outside the door.

"Almost nothing," the psychiatrist replied.

"Surely it wasn't a coincidence, her coming here before her arrest."

"Can you imagine?" the psychiatrist replied. "A chrononaut attempting to change the past?"

Wells' mind raced furiously. Somehow, Amelia had managed to survive her encounter with the Watcher. Now she'd been taken into custody.

They'll never believe her, Wells realized, remembering his own futile attempt to convince the agency of what had happened to Rebecca. They would brand Amelia insane, lock her away, and there would be no one to save her family.

He stared at the largest portrait of the Watcher for what felt like an eternity, his eyes boring into the dark lines he had violently etched into the sheet. Wells crossed the room and tore the portrait from the wall, revealing a hidden device concealed within a hole in the wall. He slid the device onto his wrist like a bracelet, hesitated, and hit a button on its flat surface.

Then he vanished from the room.

Amelia sat in the darkness of the interrogation room, waiting. She wasn't sure how much time had elapsed since the temporal enforcers pulled her out of the timestream.

I don't understand, she thought. Before, the Watcher's interference with her EMV's communications software had blinded the agency to what went on inside the timestream. Somehow when she had appeared in Eric's room, the Watcher's interference faded, allowing the agency to observe her in the present.

Did it let me escape? Amelia wondered. It didn't make sense. If the entity wanted to consume her, as Wells suggested, it couldn't do so if she was trapped in the present, unable to return to the timestream.

She shifted uneasily in her chair. The electro-magnetic

handcuffs held her hands restrained against the interview table's metal surface. *I have to get out of here,* she thought.

The door opened, and Amelia peered through the dim light to the room's entrance. In walked Herostratus. He sat opposite her, wearing a leering grin.

"How the mighty have fallen," he said, studying her with a cold gaze. "You have the agency in quite an uproar, Dr. Lewis. You're the first government-sanctioned time traveler in history to try to alter history."

"What do you want, Herostratus?" she asked.

He chuckled. "I've come to gloat, of course. The Seven Wonders Project has been temporarily suspended during the investigation into your misdeeds, but when it resumes I expect to take over your responsibilities."

Amelia huffed. *I don't have time for this.* "There are more important things than your ego, Herostratus," she said.

He raised an eyebrow. "Like the monstrous entity you claim to have seen?"

She didn't flinch from his gaze. "The Watcher is real," she said. "It's haunting time travelers who attract its attention." She leaned across the table. "Every chrononaut is in danger. Even you."

Herostratus' smile faded. Before he could reply, the door opened again, and Director Eldirch entered the interrogation room.

"Director," Herostratus said courteously, rising from the chair. He nodded at her and left without a word.

Eldrich looked down at Amelia for several seconds while standing, like a disappointed parent struggling to decide the best course to correct an errant child.

"I demand to speak with my representative," Amelia said, refusing to flinch under the director's gaze.

Eldrich folded her arms across her chest. "You've broken the cardinal rule of time travel. You have no rights, Dr. Lewis." She sat down and continued without a pause. "I'm not going to smooth over the details of what will happen to you. After we're satisfied in the answers you provide, your memories will be forcibly examined and extracted, and you'll end up in a cold, dark place for the rest of your life."

"Then why are you here?" Amelia asked.

"Because I want to know why," Eldrich answered. "You had one of the most exemplary records in the history of this agency, and you threw it all away in an attempt to save your brother's life."

"What do you mean 'attempt?'"

Eldrich shook her head. "You didn't honestly think we would allow you to successfully alter the course of events? Even if your actions wouldn't have unleashed chaos on the primary timeline, that is not a precedent I will not allow being set."

"What are you saying?" Amelia demanded.

"The moment you were taken into custody, the temporal enforcers extracted your brother's memory of your sudden appearance. He took his life later that day, the same as he did from the beginning. Your actions changed nothing, Dr. Lewis."

"You monsters," Amelia spat, her hands trembling inside her restraints.

"None of this is personal," Eldrich said. "I am sorry for what happened to your brother, but you of all people should understand that the timeline must be preserved."

Amelia paused. *She remembers my brother,* she thought. *Eldrich knows he existed.* That meant the Watcher hadn't erased him yet. But why? The answer was clear: it wasn't finished with her yet.

"I'll ask you again," Eldrich said. "Why did you do it?"

"You should have listened to me before," Amelia answered. "There's something out there—a creature that exists outside the boundaries of time and space. And it's targeted everyone I've ever loved. It's true," she insisted, seeing the skepticism on Eldrich's face. "I drew its gaze, and now it wants to devour me."

"And for the sake of the argument, just how did you draw the gaze of this creature?"

Amelia sighed and stared at the table. "I've been using my missions to observe my past," she admitted. "I haven't changed anything," she added quickly. "I just wanted to see my family again, the way it used to be."

There was a mixture of sympathy and dissatisfaction on the director's face. "How did you manage to conceal this from us?"

"You're not listening to me," Amelia protested. "That thing is out there, and it's not going to stop with me."

Eldrich stood up. "Our best researchers are going over your EMV. We'll find out how you hid the evidence of these unsanctioned trips into the past and prevent it from happening again." She sighed. "I believe something happened to you."

"You do?" Amelia asked hopefully.

"I think the stress of this job proved too much for you. You've obviously gone through a great deal of personal tragedy, and the trauma was too much to cope with." She turned to leave.

"Wait!" Amelia called out. "You have to let me go."

Eldrich glanced over her shoulder. "If it were up to me, you would have a chance at rehabilitation if you prove cooperative with our investigation. Unfortunately, there's nothing I can do. You're in the hands of the government now." She turned to leave. "Goodbye, Dr. Lewis."

Amelia listened to the sound of the door closing, trapping her alone in the room once again.

"It can't end this way," she said softly.

"Don't worry," a voice replied. "It won't."

Amelia looked up, startled, and watched as a temporal enforcer appeared inside the interrogation room. The chrononaut removed his helmet, revealing the face of Agent Wells.

"Wells," she exclaimed, surprised. "What are you doing here?"

"Getting you out of here," he said, using an electric tuner

to unlock her restraints. "We have to move quickly," he said. "It won't take long before they notice you're gone, and then the facility will go into lockdown."

"I don't understand," Amelia said. "How did you escape? And how did you get in here?"

He showed her a small device. "It's a homemade valance-phaser," he said. "I tucked it away when I was committed, just in case. I've kept it safe for all these years." He took it and slid it around her wrist. "Take it," he said.

"Why did you come back?" she asked.

"Because of you," he said. "You reminded me what it was to fight for something. The Watcher took Rebecca from me, but there's still a chance we can save your family."

"We?"

He nodded. "Maybe if we work together, we have a chance at defeating it. Now come on," he said, stretching out his hand.

Amelia took it, and when they went intangible together, he was still visible to her. They passed through the walls of the interrogation room and past the guards, climbed several sets of stairs, moving along until they were out of sight.

"We don't have much time," Amelia said when she turned off her device. "I need a suit."

"How are we going to get our hands on another EMV?" Wells asked, peering around a corner. "I took mine from the temporal enforcers' subbasement, but that's the first place they'll look for us. Aren't the suits you use kept under constant surveillance?"

"All except for one," she said, thinking on her feet. "Eldrich told me the scientists were analyzing my suit. The visor is cracked and I'm down to one temporal stabilizer, but it'll do the job. Follow me."

Sure enough, Amelia's EMV had been left abandoned in one of the research wings. Wells helped her into the familiar white and gray suit.

"Here," he said, handing her a plasma gun. "I took these when I put on my EMV. They might not affect the Watcher, but it's better than going in unarmed."

"Thanks," she said.

"Don't thank me yet," he replied, showing her how to fire the weapon. "None of this matters if we can't gain access to a time portal. Someone has to turn on the machine."

Amelia slid the gun into a holster on the suit's belt. "I think I might know just the person," she said.

It didn't take long to find Gavin. He was alone inside the room where they'd planned and coordinated so many missions together. He was pouring through files on the agency database, and video feeds of Amelia's missions played on the monitors. He looked sad, hurt even, and Amelia realized that perhaps she hadn't been alone all along. She'd had friends right under her nose, but she'd been too focused on her feelings of isolation to notice them.

"Gavin," she said, switching off the valence-phaser.

He nearly fell backward, surprised.

"Amelia," he whispered, as if unable to believe she was really there. "You escaped."

She nodded, holding her helmet in her hands so she could look him in the eyes. "I have to finish it, Gavin. My family still needs me."

Gavin's eyes wandered over to the communications system at the heart of a nearby table, as if he was debating whether or not to alert the agency to Amelia's presence.

"You broke the rules," he said. "You tried to change the past."

"I was trying to stop the Watcher," she replied. "It's real, Gavin. And it's not going to stop."

"It's true," Wells added, materializing beside her. "Agent Wells," he said by way of introduction.

Amelia laid a hand on Gavin's shoulder. "I don't know if we can stop it, Gavin, but we have to try. Please," she said. "We can't open up the portal on our own. We'd never make it in time."

Gavin sighed. "We don't have long. I can access a control room long enough to open a portal in one of the gateway chambers, but you have to get there before they shut me down. Once you enter the portal, it'll be too late for them to stop you."

Wells nodded. "Come on," he said to Amelia, and he turned to leave.

Amelia stood there for a moment longer. "Thank you, Gavin," she said.

He offered her a slight smile. "I trust you, Dr. Lewis. Now go."

As they ran down the stairs, making their way toward the heart of the facility, an alarm roared across the building. The alarm grew louder with each second, accompanied by flashing red lights.

"They know you're free," Wells said. "It won't be long before they find us."

"The elevator won't work while we're intangible," Amelia said. "It's a precautionary failsafe."

Guards were waiting for them outside the elevators that led to the bowels of the facility. From a position unseen, Gavin opened the elevator doors remotely, and Amelia and Wells raced toward it, firing at the guards with their plasma guns. The guards scattered long enough for Amelia and Wells to dive inside, and the elevator began its steep descent.

"This is an emergency," a voice echoed across the base. "Two unsanctioned individuals are attempting unauthorized access to the gateway chamber."

When the elevator doors slid open, guards were standing outside, guns pointed ahead. Amelia and Wells charged forward, intangible, and vanished through the entrance into the sealed chamber.

Amelia stared ahead at the end of the platform, her heart pounding. She hooked her tether in place, and Wells did the same.

"I hope your friend was telling the truth," Wells said, looking back at the chamber's entrance as alarms continued to sound.

The room grew dark as gusts of wind burst from the rapidly opening vortex. The doors behind them opened, and guards spilled into the chamber, but it was too late.

Amelia nodded to Wells, and they jumped into the portal and vanished.

CHAPTER EIGHT

T HEY EMERGED FROM THE VORTEX side by side, hovering in place. Amelia descended until her feet hit the tunnel floor.

"EMV synchronization initializing," the A.I. said, and her EMV's display feed—distorted by the damage sustained by her visor—split in two.

"What's happening?" she asked.

"You've never made the jump with another chrononaut before," Wells said, touching down beside her. "Our suits are synchronizing. We'll be able to track one another through time."

"Maybe," Amelia muttered. The Watcher had a way of interfering with her communications systems. She stared ahead at the timestream's expanse, searching for a sign of the entity.

Her suit was damaged from her previous encounter with the Watcher. Her primary temporal stabilizer had been compromised, which was far more serious than a shattered visor. Amelia took out the weapon she'd carried through the gateway and powered it up. Wells did the same. The plasma guns glowed with pulsing, purple light, a sign of their deadly power.

"Stay close," she said to Wells, and she motioned for him to follow. She wondered if his silence implied second thoughts about his decision to accompany her. Having left the safety of the asylum to return to the timestream, he was once again susceptible to the creature that had haunted his thoughts for years.

They advanced through the timestream, keeping their guns

pointed squarely ahead. Their path led them farther and farther from the gateway until it was no longer visible.

"Where are you hiding?" Wells said, looking around.

It suddenly occurred to Amelia that the Watcher might have allowed her to escape back to the present so that Wells might join her. Now both its intended victims were exactly where it wanted them. She wondered who was actually doing the hunting.

The cracked visor began to fog over as an overwhelming sense of cold spread through her suit.

"It's here," Wells said, his voice echoing over her radio.

The Watcher waited for them ahead. Amelia took aim with her gun, and Wells did the same.

"Be careful," she said.

The windows into the past filled with images again, but this time they were not of her brother, her father, or Collin—they were all of her. Each window showed Amelia as she journeyed into her past.

It wants me to know what it's punishing me for, she realized.

Beside her, Wells pulled the trigger of his gun, and Amelia quickly did the same. The Watcher vanished, and the blasts of energy vanished down the path.

Amelia spun around, and they stood back to back, surveying the tunnel. "Do you see anything?" she asked.

Wells didn't answer.

Amelia looked over her shoulder and saw him staring beyond the tunnel's walls. A woman with red hair floated in the ethereal gray pallor outside time and space. Amelia recognized her as Rebecca, the woman from Wells' portraits. Rebecca beckoned toward Wells, bidding him closer, and he began walking toward the edge of the path.

Amelia gazed past Rebecca and saw the Watcher hovering behind her, observing Wells.

"Wait!" Amelia called out, but he kept walking like a man

transfixed. "Wait!" she yelled, but her EMV's communication system began to malfunction.

When she started toward Wells, the Watcher reappeared inside the timestream. Before she could react, Amelia was thrown back, causing her to lose her grip on the weapon. She landed on the path, her gun just out of reach. As the Watcher descended on her, she hurled herself forward, seized the weapon, and fired. The burst of energy hit the entity, sending it spinning backward.

Amelia took aim again, but she noticed that Wells was now inches away from the edge of the path. With a sigh she took her aim off the Watcher and ran forward just as he took one step too many and began to fall. Amelia dove toward the ledge and grabbed his hand. She strained from the effort it took to hold him as his legs dangled over the side.

The cold grew, and she could feel the Watcher closing in behind her. She threw all her effort into helping Wells grab hold of the ledge. Just as he started to haul himself up, a shadow settled over the tunnel's blue wall, and Amelia turned around and found herself facing the Watcher.

Wells held out his plasma gun and fired, sending the Watcher spiraling again. Amelia took aim with her own gun, but the entity vanished. Amelia cursed. Unbound by the timestream, it was nearly invulnerable to attack.

Wells glanced over his shoulder and stared at Rebecca again.

"She's not real," Amelia shouted, hoping he could hear her over the static.

The Watcher exploded through the wall of the timestream, heading directly at Wells. He managed to pull the trigger just as the entity collided with him. The blast reverberated back on Wells. The Watcher was stunned and thrown back, and Wells skidded along the path before coming to rest, his EMV damaged by the burst of energy.

No, Amelia thought when she spotted the damage done to his temporal stabilizer. He reached toward her, only to vanish from the timestream.

When her own temporal stabilizer was compromised, Amelia had managed to fight her way back to the timestream using the backup, but not before being flung through time. Now Wells was faced with the same problem—if he could even find his way back.

She was alone again. Amelia looked at the spot where the Watcher had been, but it had disappeared again. Once more images of her brother began to stream on the walls.

"Amy?" a voice said, and suddenly he was there inside the timestream with her.

"Eric!" she exclaimed, dropping the gun. Before he could react, she wrapped him in a fierce embrace. Tears streamed down her face. "I'm so sorry," she said, sobbing. "I never wanted this to happen."

"What's happening?" he asked.

"You're in danger," she said. "But it's going to be okay. I'm going to keep you safe." She hugged him tightly, despite the awkwardness created by the bulky EMV. "I promise. I won't let you go."

"Amy?" Eric said, and his skin began to grow translucent. "I feel strange."

Before Amelia could say anything, he faded and disappeared, leaving her holding empty air.

"No!" she screamed, overcome. The Watcher had allowed her this moment just so it could snatch it away. This was what it planned to do to the rest of her family and friends—what the Watcher would do again and again to those unfortunate enough to draw its gaze.

Amelia howled with rage. The Watcher hovered opposite her, waiting. The end had come. She bellowed at the entity and hurled herself at it, only to be thrown on her back. She climbed to her feet only to again be forcefully hurled against the tunnel floor.

Amelia lay there, struggling to find the strength to rise as the Watcher slowly advanced toward her. She tasted blood in her mouth and realized she had bitten her lip. She rolled over and tried to push herself up, but she collapsed from exhaustion. The Watcher came to a stop, hovering over her triumphantly, and she stared past it down the length of the tunnel where the blue light darkened as the timestream stretched on without end. As she gazed beyond the Watcher at the tunnel's end, Amelia's bloodied lips curled into a smile.

"I'm sorry, Daddy," she whispered.

With shaking fingers, Amelia punched in a final set of coordinates into her gauntlet. Then she felt for the tether at her back and turned the handle ninety degrees. Before the Watcher could react, Amelia pushed herself up and looped around it, wrapping the golden cord tightly around the entity. The glowing light bound the Watcher, holding it inside the timestream and preventing it from fleeing outside the reaches of time and space.

"This is for my family," she said, tearing the backup temporal stabilizer off her wrist and tucking it between the tether and the Watcher as electricity pulsed between them. She hit the command key on her gauntlet, sending the Watcher back in time—all the way back to the beginning of time.

The timestream shook as the Watcher was dragged farther and farther into the tunnel, until at last it vanished from her sight.

"*Warning. Temporal destabilization imminent,*" said her suit's A.I., and Amelia felt her body begin to fluctuate. She'd used her final temporal stabilizer to transport the Watcher through time against its will, but without a stabilizer holding her in a single place in time, there was nothing to anchor her inside the timestream. And without the tether, there was no way for her to return to the present.

A deafening explosion sounded deeper within the tunnel, and a rush of dark blue luminescence slowly spread across the tunnel walls. Nothing—not even the Watcher—could exist before the beginning of existence.

I did it, Daddy, she thought as she felt her body come apart, and she closed her eyes and allowed herself to fade away.

Amelia opened her eyes.

She was no longer inside the timestream. She looked around, confused.

Where am I? she wondered. Everything seemed so familiar, like she had been there before.

"I love you, Amelia," a voice said, and she heard her father's voice.

She saw him sitting next to her childhood self, who was tucked into bed, and it dawned on her she was inside her favorite memory. After bouncing around the timestream, she had finally landed in this moment in time. Amelia tried to call out, but neither of them could hear her.

The girl's face brightened. "I love you, Daddy Buddy," she said, and they continued on as if nothing had changed.

When the scene ended, the memory repeated again, and a horrible truth occurred to her: she was stuck, trapped inside this fragment of the past.

Amelia tried to move, but she wasn't even aware of her own body. She could only watch as the memory played out again and again, forever.

CHAPTER NINE

ALL CONCEPT OF TIME FADED from her thoughts. There was only the memory, again and again. Amelia didn't know how many times she'd watched it unfold. Her purgatory seemed to stretch on without end. She struggled to remain self-aware.

Finally, when she was on the precipice of losing her fragile grip on sanity, Amelia heard a gentle voice echo outside the memory.

"This isn't how it ends," the voice said. A man in a golden EMV hovered behind her.

"I… know you," she said slowly, trying to remember. "Wells?"

His helmet bobbed up and down as he nodded. "I've come to take you home," he said, reaching toward her. "Take my hand. It's time to go."

Amelia hesitated. She looked back at the image of her father and her younger self one last time. Then she took his hand, and his temporal stabilizer glowed with white light.

Returning to the present was like waking up from a dream. Amelia couldn't recall much about how they had made their way back through the timestream; Wells later told her that he'd taken them back to a few minutes before they made the jump in the facility, only he'd set their destination for hundreds of miles away, squarely in the middle of nowhere.

All Amelia remembered was waking up in a green field,

surrounded by vivid shades of green and blue. Air rushed into her lungs, and she felt like a drowning victim emerging from the water. Her EMV felt heavy, and she lay quietly atop the grass, trying to process each new sensory input. She noticed Wells standing over her, blocking the sunlight, and her eyes closed.

The next time she woke up, she was in her own bed. After reorienting herself, she showered and changed her clothes. Amelia found Wells waiting for her outside the bedroom.

"You pulled me out of the time loop," she said. "How did you find me?"

"Our suits were synchronized," he answered. "Once I fixed my stabilizer, I jumped into the past and searched until I found you."

"That must have taken…"

"Forever," he finished. "I was worried there wouldn't be anything left of you to find."

"Thank you," she said, "for not giving up on me."

"Me?" He laughed. "You're the one who did it," he said, showing her an old family photograph he'd found in her room. Eric was no longer in the picture, but Sarah and their father were. "How did you manage it?"

"I wrapped the tether around the Watcher and used my temporal stabilizer to send it back infinitely through time."

Wells bowed his head and closed his eyes. "Rest easy, Rebecca," he said. "We beat it."

They remained in Amelia's home for several days, recovering from their encounter with the Watcher. Wells later explained that he'd travelled to the field rather than going back through the gateway for fear that they would be apprehended immediately upon their return. As it turned out, he worried needlessly.

"No one remembers you were ever arrested," he said. "When the Watcher erased your brother from existence, it erased the memory of your going back to save him from time. No one will remember him."

"But I'll remember," she said, making a promise to herself. *I'll never forget you, Eric.* She would carry his memory, and Collin's memory, inside her heart.

Almost everything else remained the same. She had still told Gavin and Director Eldrich about seeing the Watcher in the timestream, she had still been hospitalized, and she had still angrily confronted Herostratus.

They decided to keep what they had witnessed to themselves. With the Watcher destroyed, there was no way to prove it had ever existed. Wells was still considered an escaped inmate, and he made up his mind to disappear someplace where no one would think to look for him.

They parted at a cemetery. There were no graves in remembrance of Collin, Eric, or Rebecca. As far as the world was concerned, they had never existed. But Amelia and Wells remembered, and together they said a private goodbye to those they had loved.

"I wasted so much time in that room in the asylum. I was afraid to live my life," Wells told her when they finally said farewell.

"So was I," Amelia said. She extended her hand to him. "Good luck."

He shook her hand and smiled. "It's not your fault," he said. "You shouldn't blame yourself."

"I broke the rules," she replied. "I drew the Watcher's gaze. That doesn't make it fair that Collin and Eric were erased, but I have to live with it. But the truth is... I think I'm ready to. Live, that is."

Amelia resigned from the agency. She was offered several prestigious teaching posts, all of which she declined. She had earned more money than she could ever use in her time with the agency, and now she planned to use those funds to live for more than the past.

***

One other thing had changed.

Amelia's sister no longer had any memory of their brother, and as Amelia was surprised to discover, this also meant she had no memory of their falling out. Although Amelia's time as a chrononaut had placed a distance between them, there were no longer any feelings of bitterness and resentment. And with trepidation and baited breath, Amelia reached out to her sister.

Shortly thereafter, they visited their father—together.

And time marched on, much as it always had and always would.

ALTERNATE ENDING

CHAPTER SIX

S HE ALWAYS MADE THE WALK alone.

Amelia waited as the elevator began its descent, secure in her EMV. She carried her helmet in her hands. She breathed in and out calmly, her pulse steady. As the elevator plunged toward the facility's depths, she felt the seconds ticking away one by one.

Caution, an automated voice said when the elevator came to a stop. *You are entering a restricted area.*

The doors opened, and Amelia walked down a solitary hallway toward the entrance to the gateway chamber. She heard Gavin say something over her receiver, but it hardly registered. Her focus was on the task at hand.

She stopped briefly outside the entrance, where two guards stood watch. Amelia submitted to a retinal scan, and somewhere Gavin entered a complementary sequence to open the impenetrable doors. Amelia passed between the guards without a word and stepped over the threshold into the massive dome-shaped chamber. When the doors shut behind her, she lowered the helmet over her head and fastened it into place. She didn't look back.

Amelia's footsteps echoed softly off the walls of the quiet chamber. She advanced toward the platform at the heart of the chamber, which had already started to glow from the light gathering across the metallic archway. The gateway chamber hummed with a silent energy from the fusion reactor buried under the waters below. The energy coursed through the walls into the archway at the end of the platform.

Before Amelia reached the end of the walkway, she retrieved the tether, slid it into position in the back of her suit, and locked it in place. As she continued her approach, the golden cord also began to ebb with light.

"Gateway commencement in five," a random technician's voice echoed through the chamber. "Four."

This is it, Amelia thought. There was no turning back now— at least not for her.

"Three."

As the technician's voice continued the countdown, Amelia thought not of herself, but of those she loved. Her clenched fists shook not with fear, but with resolve. Her face glowed with an expression of determination in the gathering illumination.

"Two."

One by one, the features of her suit were highlighted as the EMV ran a pre-jump test for functionality.

Tether engaged. Temporal stabilizers activated. Valence-phaser ready. A.I. and communications systems are online.

"One."

A vortex opened under the archway, growing in size until it covered half the platform. Generated currents swept across the chamber, howling off the walls like vengeful spirits. The room darkened as most of the light was absorbed by the vortex, save for the tether's golden illumination. Amelia stood facing the portal—black surrounded by a cone of overpowering light—and bowed her head.

"Dr. Lewis, you are cleared to enter the timestream," Gavin's voice sounded in her helmet.

She stared up at the gateway, nodded firmly, and jumped into the vortex.

The sensation was always the same—the brief interlude of

overpowering white light, followed by the utter loneliness of the abyss in the moments before she emerged on the other side of the portal.

After saying goodbye to her father, she'd tried her best to come up with a way to defeat the Watcher. Every idea seemed more futile than the last, and if Wells' story was anything to go on, she didn't have that much time until the entity began removing more people from her life. So she decided to give the Watcher what it wanted: her. Either she would defeat it, and in doing so save her family, or it would erase her as Wells foretold, in which case it would no longer need to wipe her loved ones from existence. One way or another, it would end today.

Amelia had returned to work after what felt like an appropriate length of time to recover from her previous encounter with the watcher. She was careful to avoid arousing suspicion about her motives, and as such had apologized both to Director Eldrich and Gavin for what she claimed to have witnessed, attributing the watcher to an injury-induced hallucination. That seemed to satisfy both of them, although smoothing things over with Eldrich about her attack on Herostratus proved more difficult. Amelia used the stress over her ordeal to her advantage and offered Herostratus a place on the team, which finally cleared the way for her return to active duty. After that, it was all a matter of preparing for her next journey into the past and readying herself to face what lay ahead.

If I make it through this, she promised herself, *things are going to be different.* Amelia was finished living in the past. She realized now how much she wanted to live, and how much she still had to live for.

Amelia passed through the vortex, the tether's golden light glowing behind her. On the other side, she hovered just outside the gateway, watching the timestream's otherworldly blue light through her visor.

"Temporal flux stabilized," Gavin's voice echoed over her receiver. "Dr. Lewis, do you copy?"

Amelia didn't answer. She landed on the tunnel floor and gazed across the vast expanse of the timestream. The tunnel appeared much as it always had; the blue light pulsed under her feet with each step she took, and the white windows interspersed across the walls glowed rhythmically, like mirrors struck by a snowstorm. She looked from side to side, searching for something out of place. The timestream was empty, but Amelia knew she wasn't alone.

"Dr. Lewis?" Gavin repeated. "Amelia? Do you copy?"

Again she remained silent. She peered past the tunnel walls at the gray twilight beyond.

"I know you're there," she said. "Show yourself."

Suddenly, a deep, penetrating cold spread through the timestream, and Amelia's body shivered involuntarily. The images displayed by her visor began to twist and distort.

"Amelia?" Gavin asked, and his words grew disjointed as static enveloped the receiver. "We're having trouble establishing a visual connection. What's happening?"

"Tell my father and sister I love them," Amelia said before the transmission cut out, unsure if he'd heard her. Then she turned off the communications system, and the sound of static was replaced by the silence of the timestream.

Without warning, the watcher descended through the roof of the tunnel. Amelia, who had been expecting it to attack from either side, was caught off guard. She stumbled back and landed on the floor. The monolithic watcher took up almost the entire height of the tunnel. It stopped, hovering in place above her, and Amelia used the opportunity to quickly push herself to her feet. She faced the creature with defiance in her heart.

"Leave my family out of this," she said. "This is between you and me."

The watcher didn't respond. She didn't even know if it could speak, or if it was capable of speech. Instead, the windows into the past all glowed at once, and to Amelia's horror began playing images of her brother's life. She saw him as an infant, a young boy, and an adult as the moments of his life played out before her eyes, each window in an endless loop.

Amelia screamed with rage and took out the weapon she'd brought with her through the gateway—a plasma gun the temporal enforcers carried with them to neutralize unauthorized time travelers. She aimed at the watcher, but before she could fire, the entity vanished from the timestream. Amelia took a step back, glancing from side to side. She fought the urge to panic. Where had it gone?

She caught a glimpse of something outside the tunnel's walls, and Amelia remembered that the watcher existed beyond time and space.

As long as it's out there, I can't hurt it, she thought, searching for where it was hiding—if it was even hiding at all. Then she spotted it, watching her from the gray ether. Amelia approached the blue wall slowly, her gun trained in front of her, careful to avoid getting too close to the edge.

"What are you playing at?" she demanded.

Suddenly, the watcher vanished again, this time reappearing behind her. Amelia spun around, but it was too late. The watcher collided with her, and she felt herself lifted off the ground. She crashed hard against the tunnel floor, and the gun went sliding off along the floor, all as images of her brother continued to stream on the walls. Amelia lunged for the gun and grabbed it just as the watcher approached. Again the entity vanished, and the blast from her gun vanished down the timestream.

Amelia stumbled to her feet, shaken by the impact. With nothing holding it in place, the watcher was almost impossible to hit. In contrast, she was exposed and vulnerable to attack. She felt a sudden burst of coldness behind her, and again she was lifted off her feet. This time she was thrown against the tunnel's roof. She dropped the gun and landed hard on the floor. Before she could reach for the weapon, she was hurled backward, partially shattering her visor.

The watcher hit her again and again, battering her and keeping her off step.

"EMV integrity compromised," her suit's A.I. announced, and the next time she was struck, Amelia felt the primary temporal stabilizer on her chest break when she landed facedown.

Oh no, she thought. Her twin stabilizers were the only things anchoring her in a specific place in time.

"Warning," the A.I. said. *"Temporal destabilization imminent."*

Amelia saw the watcher floating toward her, and rather than trying to back away, she lunged toward it. There was a pulse of electricity from her damaged stabilizer, and one of the white windows opened up and swallowed her whole.

Amelia felt herself falling through time. She concentrated and started to type coordinates into her gauntlet, but the watcher appeared behind her, following her through time. Before she could react, she was standing in an open field as primitive-looking humans on overlooking hills converged toward her, casting spears and firing arrows in her direction. Amelia tried turning on her valance-phaser, but it wouldn't respond. She fled through the field, weighed down by the EMV.

Another hole in time opened up, and Amelia was suddenly standing at the base of an active volcano. Dinosaurs killed and ate each other upon the desolate rock, and she battled to stay upright as violent tremors ripped through the blackened earth. One of the raptors spotted Amelia and began chasing her, its jaws open in hungry anticipation. She finally managed to turn on the valance-phaser moments before it reached her.

Then she disappeared again. She felt herself sinking in the

unfathomable depths of the ocean, surrounded by darkness everywhere. The watcher was nowhere to be seen.

Why didn't it follow me? Amelia thought. Her mind flashed back to the images playing on the tunnel walls, and she knew why. It was going after her brother.

Amelia punched in a set of coordinates to her gauntlet to a date she had never forgotten—the day of her brother's suicide.

Please, let this work, she thought desperately. The remaining temporal stabilizer on her wrist kicked in, and she felt herself pulled through time and space one more time.

She was standing inside a room she recognized as her brother's, and there he was. Amelia was overcome. She had always avoided returning to her memories of him as an adult, and that day of all days in particular. Amelia reached toward him, but he didn't notice her, and she remembered she was invisible to him.

There was always a moment in time someone wanted to change. Time travelers were no different. So many times before Amelia had wished she could go back and prevent her father from contracting his illness or her brother from having killed himself. Although she was a chrononaut, she was still a human being. But Amelia understood why the use of time travel to alter the past was restricted. If everyone tried to go back, the timeline would be irreversibly damaged, perhaps broken altogether.

And yet, as she watched her brother, Amelia knew she had to do something. *I won't let it take him,* she thought. She knew the rules. She understood what would happen if she tried to alter the past, but she no longer cared.

"Eric?" she said, turning off the valence-phaser.

Her brother jumped, shocked by her sudden appearance. "Amy?" he asked, visibly confused.

Amelia felt a lump forming in her throat. How many times had she wished for this—for one last chance to say goodbye. A chance to make things right.

Before Eric could react, she wrapped him in a fierce embrace. Tears streamed down her eyes. "I'm so sorry," she said, sobbing. "I never wanted this to happen."

"What's happening?" he asked.

"You're in danger," she said. "But it's going to be okay. I'm going to keep you safe." She hugged him tightly, despite the awkwardness created by the bulky EMV. "I promise. I won't let you go."

Slowly, the possessions in Eric's room began to flicker and fade one by one into nothingness.

"Amy?" Eric said, and his skin began to grow translucent. "I feel strange."

Before Amelia could say anything, he faded and disappeared, leaving her holding empty air.

"No!" she screamed, her helmet flooded with tears. The watcher had allowed her this moment just so it could snatch it away. This was what it planned to do to the rest of her family and friends—what the watcher would do again and again to those unfortunate enough to draw its gaze.

Amelia howled with rage as the scene dissolved around her, leaving her standing once more inside the timestream, surrounded by the constant rotation of the blue walls. The watcher hovered opposite her, waiting. The end had come.

She bellowed at the entity and hurled herself at it, only to be thrown on her back. Amelia lay there, struggling to find the strength to rise as the watcher slowly advanced toward her. She rolled over and tried to push herself up, but she collapsed from exhaustion. The watcher came to a stop, hovering over her triumphantly, and she stared past it down the length of the tunnel where the blue light darkened as the timestream stretched on without end. As she gazed beyond the watcher at the tunnel's end, Amelia's bloodied lips curled into a smile.

"I'm sorry, Daddy," she whispered.

With shaking fingers, Amelia punched in a final set of

coordinates into her gauntlet. Then she felt for the tether at her back and turned the handle ninety degrees. Before the watcher could react, Amelia pushed herself up and looped around it, wrapping the golden cord tightly around the entity. The glowing light bound the watcher, holding it inside the timestream and preventing it from fleeing outside the reaches of time and space.

"This is for my family," she said, tearing the backup temporal stabilizer off her wrist and attaching it to the watcher as electricity pulsed between them. She hit the command key on her gauntlet, sending the watcher back in time—all the way back to the beginning of time.

The timestream shook as the watcher was dragged farther and farther into the tunnel, until at last it vanished from her sight.

"*Warning. Temporal destabilization imminent,*" said her suit's A.I., and Amelia felt her body begin to fluctuate. She'd used her final temporal stabilizer to transport the watcher through time against its will, but without a stabilizer holding her in a single place in time, there was nothing to anchor her inside the timestream. And without the tether, there was no way for her to return to the present.

A deafening explosion sounded deeper within the tunnel, and a rush of dark blue luminescence slowly spread across the tunnel walls. Nothing—not even the watcher—could exist before the beginning of existence.

I did it, daddy, she thought as she felt her body come apart, and she closed her eyes and allowed herself to fade away.

Days later, Amelia's sister Sarah attended her funeral with their father. No one at the agency could tell them what had happened to her. They didn't know themselves, and were little closer to finding the truth, even after launching an extensive internal investigation. Detailed reviews discovered that Amelia had used time travel for personal reasons over the course of her missions, but there was no evidence that she had attempted to alter the past. Because her communications systems had malfunctioned, there was no record of what had happened to her inside the timestream, only a thousand different theories.

But since the watcher hadn't erased Amelia from existence, she was not forgotten. Gavin remembered what she had said about the thing she saw inside the timestream, and how she had sought out former Agent Wells. After talking to Wells himself, he began to wonder for the first time about the possibility Amelia had been telling the truth.

And time marched on, much as it always had and always would.

Amelia opened her eyes.

She was no longer inside the timestream. She looked around, confused.

Where am I? she wondered. Everything seemed so familiar, like she had been there before.

"I love you, Amelia," a voice said, and she heard her father's voice.

She saw him sitting next to her childhood self, who was tucked into bed, and it dawned on her she was inside her favorite memory. After bouncing around the timestream, she had finally landed in this moment in time. Amelia tried to call out, but neither of them could hear her.

The girl's face brightened. "I love you, daddy buddy," she said, and they continued on as if nothing had changed.

When the scene ended, the memory repeated again, and a horrible truth occurred to her: she was stuck, trapped inside this fragment of the past.

Amelia tried to move, but she wasn't even aware of her own body. She could only watch as the memory played out again and again, forever.

AFTERWORD

Haven't you ever wanted to go back? I know I have.

This story evolved far beyond my original plans, as stories are wont to do. When I started, I really just wanted to tell a good monster story. When I set out to create my monster, I thought about the most crucial element of horror—the fear of the unknown. As a species we continually strive to push beyond the limits of our understanding, until what was previously unknown becomes the known. Early seafarers feared what lurked beneath the depths, and so on.

With this in mind, the idea of time travel as a next frontier of sorts came to me, and the basic concept for this story was born. The blend of horror and science fiction seemed natural. I made a point to actively ignore scientific theories related to time travel, like the grandfather paradox or the existence of parallel worlds, because ultimately, the mechanics of time travel are really irrelevant to the message the story is trying to convey.

And it was that message that made the story so radically different than what I originally envisioned. For me, it's about much more than the haunting of a time traveler.

It wasn't until I saw a twenty-year-old video of my sister as a little girl, sharing the most beautiful smile in the world with her "daddy buddy," that the heart of the story took shape.

Like my protagonist, I'm someone sorely tempted by the allure of the past. Living in the present is a difficult business, and as a writer, it's already easy enough to slip into fantasy. In many ways, Amelia and I aren't so very different from one another. I've always viewed my youth as a golden age; it's the time when my entire family was together under one roof, until we grew up and life took us in different directions, as it does for everyone.

I know what it is to hurt the people I care about, with or without noble intent. I know what it is to lose friendships, and know it was because of something I did. I know what it is to have left things unsaid. I know what it is to wish there was a way to take a choice back—a way to make everything like it was before.

But as tempting as it may be, living in the past can also be a dangerous preoccupation, as Amelia discovered for herself. On the day you wake up and realize you're truly alone…well, I imagine there are few greater feelings of sadness than that—especially if you've known happiness before.

Luckily, that depressing note isn't the end of the story. Or at least it doesn't have to be. It took being haunted to make Amelia wake up and realize what was important in her life. The great thing about living in the present is that nothing is set in stone. The past can't be changed, after all, but the future can. You don't have to do today what you did yesterday. There is always the chance of a new beginning. And that's what makes life worth living.

ACKNOWLEDGMENTS

I want to thank everyone who played a role in the production of this novella. First and foremost I want to thank the members of my family who read the story first: Pam, Robert, Megan, and Allie. Your feedback and suggestions are invaluable to me. I couldn't do any of this without your support.

I would like to thank Christopher Hastings for introducing me to the term 'chrononaut' for time travelers in the pages of *Dr. McNinja*. Without you I wouldn't have my title!

I also want to thank my editors, Dr. Susan Wright and Amanda Lee. This is my first self-published work, and it was important to me to be sure the manuscript was reviewed as carefully as it would have been by any in-house editor at any publishing house. Fortunately for me, they are more than equal to the task. I feel confident in knowing that they painstakingly combed through each mistake, be it grammatical or structural.

I also want to thank the production team that put the novella together, including cover and interior formatting.

In addition, I would like to thank everyone who made my first published book, *The Keeper of the Crows*, a success. It continues to perform better than I ever hoped, and it's all thanks to you! Special thanks to Marsha Grant, Donna Grammer, Suzanne Rush, Joan Deane Risen, Carol Perkins, Susan Chambers, Laura Rogers, Tammy Willis, Kelli Estes, and so many more. From newspaper to radio to book signings and even television, it's been one heck of a ride so far!

And as always, thank you for reading. I hope you enjoyed this story. This is my first novella-length work, and I think the format fit the story's pacing perfectly. If you liked it, please let me know by leaving a review on Amazon or Goodreads!

If you are interested in reading more by me, be sure to check my website, www.kylealexanderromines.com, for a list of all my books currently available for purchase. You can also sign up to receive email updates about my latest endeavors. And of course, feel free to contact me if you wish to discuss this story or anything else.

Thanks again,
Kyle

ABOUT THE AUTHOR

Kyle Alexander Romines is a teller of tales from the hills of Kentucky. He enjoys good reads, thunderstorms, and anything edible. His writing interests include fantasy, science fiction, horror, and western.

Kyle's lifelong love of books began with childhood bedtime stories and was fostered by his parents and teachers. He grew up reading *Calvin and Hobbes*, RL Stine's *Goosebumps* series, and *Harry Potter*. His current list of favorites includes Justin Cronin's *The Passage*, *Hard Country* by Michael McGarrity, *Red Rising* by Pierce Brown, and *Bone* by Jeff Smith. The library is his friend.

Kyle discovered a passion for writing after graduating high school, which resulted in the completion of three novel length manuscripts before *The Keeper of the Crows*, his first published novel. These fledgling attempts at writing taught him a great deal, and since writing *Keeper* he has worked to continue honing his skills. He hopes to keep writing as long as he has stories to tell.

His next novel-length work, a western, has been accepted for publication by Sunbury Press.

You can contact Kyle at thekylealexander@hotmail.com, or visit his website at www.kylealexanderromines.com.

58223800R00068

Made in the USA
Middletown, DE
19 December 2017